MUSCADINE WINE

BY
MILTON J. DAVIS

MVmedia, LLC
Fayetteville, Georgia

MVmedia, LLC
PO Box 1465
Fayetteville, GA 30214
www.mvmediaalt.com

Publisher's Note: This is a work of fiction. Names, characters, places, and incidents are a product of the author's imagination. Locales and public names are sometimes used for atmospheric purposes. Any resemblance to actual people, living or dead, or to businesses, companies, events, institutions, or locales is completely coincidental.

Book Layout ©2017BookDesignTemplates.com
Cover art by Elizabeth Leggett
Cover design by Uraeus

Ordering Information:
Quantity sales. Special discounts are available on quantity purchases by corporations, associations, and others. For details, contact the "Special Sales Department" at the address above.

Muscadine Wine/Milton J. Davis. –1st ed.
ISBN 979-8-9857336-3-1

CONTENTS

3

To The Family

Johnson's Farm

They came for Cody Johnson on a moonless night after a summer downpour. Fog covered their approach through the pines, mist rising like steam from the grass, the air so humid it was hard to breathe. Every man creeping across the wet ground had no remorse for what they were about to do. Niggers needed to know their place. They ought not strive for what they didn't deserve. The men felt justified in what they were about to do.

But Cody Johnson wasn't a fool. He slept with double-barrel shotgun by his bed and a Colt revolver under his pillow. His hound dogs were trained to howl when the wind blew hard. He knew they would come for him sooner or later. And when they did, he'd be ready. The dogs wailed and Johnson sat up in his bed. He grabbed his coveralls and shimmied into them. Cody took the Colt from under his pillow and put it in his right-hand pocket. Grabbing the shotgun, he ambled over to his bedroom window, the window that faced the woods behind the farm. The fog made it hard to see, but the dogs made it clear they were coming that way.

"I knows y'all out there!" Johnson shouted. "And I know why y'alls here. I'm giving y'all one chance to go on back home. One chance!"

The men kept coming. They thought there was no way Johnson would fire on them. He was signing his death sentence if he did.

Johnson went to his cabinet and got the shotgun shells. He was dead no matter what he did. But he wasn't leaving this world alone. He loaded the double-barrel then cocked back the hammers.

"One last chance!" he shouted.

7

Silas Cane, county deputy sheriff and wizard of the local Ku Klux Klan had about enough of Johnson. He stood up straight, making himself seen.

"Shut up, nigger!" he shouted back. "You know good and damn well . . ."

Johnson fired both barrels into Silas's chest. The man flew back twenty feet then rolled until he stopped at the forest edge, dead as a doornail.

The other men pulled out guns and fired back as they fled for the woods, killing Cody's hounds. Johnson kept loading and shooting until he was out of shells. He took out the revolver and shot more, striking Billy Wayne-wright in the knee, crippling the butcher for life.

When Johnson finally ran out of bullets the Klan rushed in. Malcolm Coldwater was the first through the door. Johnson hit him square across the mouth with the shotgun butt. Malcolm fell to the ground cussing through his ruined teeth as the other men jumped over him and set about beating Johnson unconscious. Some of the men wanted to kill him right then and there, but Thom Crowder, president of Crowder County Banking and Savings wouldn't allow it. He was senior commander since Silas got blown to hell.

"We came to make an example out of this boy," he said. "And that's what we're going to do!"

They dragged Cody's unconscious body out of the house then loaded him into the back of Tim Foley's Ford pickup. The illicit caravan sped through the night to the massive red oak standing by the bank of Poor Man's Creek. They threw water on Johnson's face until he re-vived, tied a rope around his neck then strung it to a low, thick branch on the tree.

"You asked for this, nigger!" Thom Crowder shouted. The men cheered his words. Johnson glared at them all, not one ounce of fear in his eyes.

"You sorry ass crackers come to take my land because you ain't good enough to build something for yourself. But I swear before God Almighty ain't nan one of you will ever live on my land. It's mine now, and it always will be!"

Johnson ended his words with a wad of spit that landed on Thom Crowder's shoe. Thom gave Tim the signal and Tim sped away. Johnson dropped, but the men didn't get the show they were expecting. Johnson hung rigid like a slab of meat in the smokehouse, glaring until the life left his eyes. Someone from the crowd doused his body with kerosene and lit it afire, the men watching Johnson burn until the rope broke and the flaming body fell to the ground. The area was swept with a gust of wind that carried Johnson's ashes into the crowd, stinging the spectators' eyes and chilling them like a winter gale. The men hurried away; their nefarious deed done.

The sheriff waited three days before sending his deputies to investigate the 'disturbance' at the Johnson Farm. They walked around the house then returned to the station to file their bogus report. The Johnson farm was put up for sale, since Johnson was never married, and his kinfolks were too afraid to claim what belonged to them. An auction was held two weeks after Johnson's disappearance. A few colored farmers tried to take part but were run off by the sheriff and his deputies. Thom Crowder placed the highest bid, and The Johnson Farm became a part of his growing farming empire, added to his traditional family farm and the other land he'd acquired by foreclosure and paying delinquent taxes.

Thom paid a visit to the farm the next day. He was always impressed by Johnson's property. Cody did a good job keeping it productive, especially for a colored man. The fields were always neatly plowed and the harvests plentiful. His livestock was healthy and well groomed.

The truth was The Johnson Farm sat on some of the best farmland in the Georgia Heartland, blessed with timely rain and a natural spring that supplied irrigation water during dry spells. Thom had big plans for the land; he was going to plant the largest peach grove the state had ever seen.

He was walking back to his car when he heard a strange sound coming from the well. Thom shuffled over with a frown. The last thing he needed was some animal falling into the water source and contaminating it. He took off his hat then peered inside, hoping to get a glimpse of the hapless beast. A freezing breeze swirled around his knees and Thom felt his feet lift from the ground. The last thing Thom Crowder saw was the sweet well water of Johnson Farm.

Mr. Crowder's funeral was a spectacle. All the bank employees attended, as well as noted county officials and members of the Klan. The governor sent his representative; he didn't care much for Thom Crowder, seeing that he almost defeated him in the last election. No colored folks were in attendance, not that they would have been allowed. The county flags were flown at half-mast for a week in honor of a man who had spent his life in service to his fellow citizens and the State of Georgia.

The Johnson Farm was up for bid again. Crowder's only son, Bocephus, was not a farmer and had no ambitions of expanding the family holdings. His daughter Darlene had long abandoned the family for the cosmopolitan life in Atlanta, and her twin Sharlene was happy teaching third grade at the county elementary school for white children. A few colored farmers showed up again, and again they were turned away. Crowder was the richest man in the county, so the bidding didn't get as high. The farm was sold to the man who drove the truck from which Cody Johnson was hanged, Tim Foley.

The Foley clan had scratched a meager living from the Georgia red clay long before the state was a state. They were simple folk; their only significant achievements were losing eight male family members during the War of Northern Aggression and protecting their farm from roving Yankees during Sherman's march to the sea. The boys usually dropped out of school at eighth grade; the girls married and started families young. But Tim was ambitious. He fought against his father's wishes and graduated with a high school diploma and dreams of a better life. Those dreams were dashed when Tim's daddy died from a gunshot wound to the head during a disagreement after a game of dice behind Mr. Pritchard's country store. Since Tim was the eldest, the responsibility for the farm and the family fell on his narrow shoulders.

The added burden failed to extinguish Tim's backwoods ambition. He found his path to fortune making moonshine, using his home-grown skill to build the largest still in the county and providing the local honkytonks with cheap spirits. The business wasn't as lucrative as he hoped; there were many hands he had to grease to keep the law looking the other way. When the Johnson Farm came up for bid again, Tim's goals were modest. He would clear the forest, selling the pines for pulpwood and the oaks for firewood. He'd divide the land into small plots and sharecrop it to white and colored folks too poor to afford their own land.

Tim drove out to the land the day after he got the deed. The farm was still in good shape despite the lack of maintenance since Johnson's killing. He used the old key to enter the house; everything was in order, although a bit musty and dusty. He opened the windows to let in the fresh summer air. He had a mind to stay the night but thought better of it. Daisy would think he was running around with Gertrude Potter. That was Wednesday nights, but Daisy wouldn't care.

He strolled to the livestock pens near the woods. The chickens were nowhere to be found, but the mule was still in its gate. Its ribs were starting to show from lack of food. Tim couldn't have any animal dying on him, at least not until he carried out his plans. He located the barn and found a pile of hay. With the pitchfork he scooped up a mound and carried it to the mule, dropping it under the mule's head. The mule ate eagerly as Tim sauntered away, lighting a cigarette. As he walked behind the mule, a teeth chattering wind blew up on him. That same wind caught a mud dauber, pushing the insect into the mule's flanks. The mud dauber stung the mule; the mule cried out in pain then kicked. Its rear hooves collided with Tim's head and sent him straight toward whatever hell he knew.

Daisy found Tim's body three days later. She called the sheriff; the deputies arrived an hour later and declared Tim's death accidental. Tim's relatives built him a fine casket and buried him in the family cemetery beside daddy and the family war heroes. Once again, his ambitions had been denied.

The Johnson Farm was up for bid again. The Foley family was too poor to maintain it, especially with Tim's untimely demise. The colored folks didn't show this time. They knew better. Johnson's Farm was meant to stay his, and although he failed to protect it in the here and now, he was doing a fine job in the next. A crowd formed on the county courthouse steps, much smaller than previously and with much less enthusiasm. The man who won the bid wasn't a county resident; he hailed from nearby Tidwell County and was unknown to everyone in attendance. He paid for the land in cash right after the auction was complete, took the deed, hurried to his car then sped away.

Billy Ray Calhoun was a respectable man, as good as a white man could be for the times. Although he was a staunch believer in white supremacy, he believed that the Negro race should be respected and allowed to accomplish whatever its limited skills could achieve. He was well aware of the strange occurrences of Johnson's Farm, but unlike others Billy had connections in the Negro community. Not only did he know what plagued the farm, he also knew the solution.

Billy hired Tommy Small to take him into nearby Cooter Swamp where Miss Hattie resided. Tommy made him pay double the price, just in case Miss Hattie cursed them both and he had to buy root remedies. It took half the day to reach the pine rise where Miss Hattie lived, a tiny island surrounded by tea-colored water and cypress trees draped with Spanish moss. Billy stepped gingerly onto the moss-covered ground and tipped toward the house. It was a beacon surrounded by the dismal, a well-made structure painted white with blue windows and a blue door to keep the haints out. A small broom leaned against an old rocking chair, another precaution for any witches that might try to enter. Billy knocked on the door.

"Is that you Billy Calhoun?" a high-pitched voice called out.

Billy hesitated before answering. He had not informed Miss Hattie of his visit.

"Ye . . . Yes, Miss Hattie! It's Billy Calhoun."

"Come on in here!"

Billy entered the house and was greeted by the smell of moth balls and jasmine. Miss Hattie's parlor was well appointed; there was no better furnished room south of Macon.

"Take a seat," Miss Hattie called out. "I'll be in directly."

Billy sat in the plush chair near the door just in case he had to make a hasty exit. Miss Hattie entered the room moments later, and Bill Calhoun was stunned. The rumors were that Miss Hattie was as old as the swamp and twice as ugly. The truth was the exact opposite. Miss Hattie stood as tall as most men, with smooth black skin and a pleasant youthful face that contrasted with silver gray hair piled atop her head. She wore a thin flowered house dress that hugged her shapely body near her breasts and hips. Miss Hattie carried a tray with two cups of steaming liquid.

"Hello, Billy," she said in a pleasant disarming tone. "Do you like what you see?"

Billy turned red as a beet. "I must say I do, Miss Hattie."

Miss Hattie chuckled. "I meant the furniture. Had it shipped all the way from New Orleans."

"Of course," Billy replied. "It's beautiful."

Miss Hattie offered Billy tea, then sat on the sofa on the opposite side of the room. Billy sipped his tea and felt a calm pass through his body. Miss Hattie grinned as if she knew what he experienced.

"This is excellent tea," he said.

"I know," Miss Hattie replied. "It was Cody's favorite. He loved it as much as he loved his land."

A chill gripped Billy as Miss Hattie uttered those words. He placed down his cup.

"That's what I'm here to discuss, Miss Hattie," he said. "You probably already know that I purchased the deed to Cody's farm."

"Mr. Johnson to you," Miss Hattie said. "You didn't know the man, and you don't have the right to call him by his first name."

"I apologize," Billy said. "I never meant to offend. People in my county know that I have always thought well of the Negro race."

"Let's get down to it," Miss Hattie said. "You want me to help you lay claim to Cody's farm. You want me to lay Cody's spirit to rest."

"Yes, I do," Billy replied. "And I'm willing to pay whatever it takes to do so."

"Five thousand dollars," Miss Hattie said.

Billy almost fell out of his chair. "What?!?"

"You heard me right,' Miss Hattie replied. "Cody never was able to get his full due from his land because of white folks, and I know full well what that land will be worth in your hands. You'll make more than enough."

Billy rubbed his chin. "Still, that's a lot of money . . ."

"For a nigger?" Miss Hattie finished. "You have a choice, Billy. Pay me and claim Cody's farm or leave."

"Mama?"

Billy looked to the source of the voice. A girl stood in the kitchen doorway, the mirror image to Miss Hattie. Miss Hattie looked at the girl and frowned.

"Go on now girl," she said. "This is grown folks' business."

"Yes, ma'am," the girl said. She glanced at Billy then backed into the darkness. Billy heard a screen door creak open then slam.

"A sweet looking child," Billy commented. "Who's her daddy?"

"That's none of your business," Miss Hattie said. "Do we have a deal?"

Billy leaned back into his chair. "Five thousand is a lot of money for anyone. But I understand what you're doing. You're looking out for yourself and your child. I think twenty-five hundred is good enough."

Miss Hattie stood. "It was nice meeting you, Billy. I wish you luck with your new farm."

Billy jumped to his feet.

"That's it? You're not open to haggling?"

"No," Miss Hattie replied. "Five thousand or nothing."

Billy surrendered. "I don't have that kind of money right now."

"When you get it, send it by Tommy," Miss Hattie said. "I'll send you what you need."

"How do I know I can trust you," Billy asked.

"You don't," Miss Hattie replied. "It's a risk you'll have to take. Goodbye, Billy. See yourself out."

Billy Calhoun left Miss Hattie's house in a quandary. He'd bought the Johnson Farm for much less than it was worth, yet Miss Hattie's deal would bring the price slightly higher than he'd planned. But he had no choice. Cody Johnson's spirit had to be quelled.

Three days after their meeting, Billy Calhoun returned to Miss Hattie's house with five thousand dollars. He knocked on the door. Instead of Miss Hattie, he was greeted by the girl. She held a burlap sack in one hand and a small box in the other.

"Mama told me to give you this," she said.

Billy took the bag and the box. He placed them on the porch then handed the girl an envelope with the money.

"You make sure your Mama gets that," he said.

The girl frowned. "I ain't no thief."

"I know," Billy said. "Tell your mama I said thank you."

Billy picked up the items and began to leave.

"Wait a minute," the girl said.

She handed Billy a folded piece of paper.

"Instructions," she said.

"Thank . . ."

The girl closed the door on him.

Billy unfolded the note and read it on his way back.

Inside the bag is another bag. After the next rain, spread the contents on the grounds as well as you can. Once that's done, build a small fire outside the barn. Take half the contents of the small box and throw it into the fire. Take the rest of it home and brew it. Sprinkle a little on your shoes, then drink the rest. Cody won't worry you no more.

Miss Hattie

Billy did as Miss Hattie instructed. The rain that soaked the farm appeared like divine intervention, a brief summer squall that released its blessing only on the farm and the nearby woods. Billy arrived on the property a few hours later, spreading the odoriferous concoction over the grounds. It took a moment to start a fire on the damp grass; once it was lit, Billy tossed half the contents of the box into the fire and was rewarded with the pleasant aroma of Miss Hattie's excellent tea. The fragrance cancelled out the contents of the bag, restoring order to the farm. Billy drove home, kissing his wife and patting his dog's head before brewing the tea. He dribbled the tea on his shoes as instructed, then spent the evening enjoying the remaining brew while reading the newspaper. Billy slept peacefully, expectant of the days ahead.

The next morning Billy's wife, Cindy, awoke and prepared breakfast. She called out for her husband, then went to find him when he didn't answer. Billy lay in the bed, a pleasant look on his face. His wife grinned, then shook her husband to wake him. His head fell at an odd angle, and his wife covered her mouth in shock. Billy Calhoun had died in his sleep with dreams of the Johnson Farm.

The county coroner announced his findings on Billy's death two weeks after it occurred. Billy had been poisoned. The first suspicion went to his wife, but everyone who knew the Calhouns vouched for Cindy and her fathomless love for her husband. Time passed and whispers became rumors. Those rumors were enough for the Klan. On a moonless night they gathered at the edge of Cooter Swamp, piled into their johnboats and set off for Miss Hattie's home. Once they reached the isolated abode, they opened fire, tearing the house apart with buck shot and 30/30 rounds. They landed their boats in an invasion of white robes, bursting into the house to see their handiwork firsthand. They were disappointed. There was no one inside; no body to claim and defile. They looted the home of whatever furniture or items undamaged by their gunfire, then set the house ablaze.

Once again Johnson's Farm was up for bid. This time, no one came. The message was clear to both Negroes and White people; Johnson's farm belonged to Cody Johnson. The land became part of county property, where it languished, nature claiming what once belonged to her. Buildings decayed and collapsed. The only structure that withstood time was Johnson's home. Though vines found purchase on the walls, the building refused to succumb. It was as if Cody Johnson was inside holding up the walls himself.

Decades came and went. The world changed and the state reluctantly conformed. The latest governor announced a highway would be built running the length of the state, and that highway would run through the county. Of course, those privy to such information quickly purchased the land the state would claim, all except Johnson's Farm. The highway came through with an army of bulldozers, levelers, and pavers, bringing a level of prosperity the county had never seen. Tax revenues swelled as did the pockets of the county officials. But due to the attention of the state and the country, the old political system was dismantled. The new liberal residents of the county clashed with the down-home folks as the county was dragged kicking and screaming into the 21st century. Through all the change and turmoil, Johnson's Farm was untouched.

* * *

One warm day in March, ten minutes after the property office of the new county government building opened for business, the old-time bell rang as a tall umber skinned woman entered the building walking with a regal stride. Her floral print dress matched the headwrap that towered over her, her matching hoop earrings and septum ring complementing her bracelets. The clerk looked at her in wonder; she was definitely not from around these parts.

"May I help you?" the clerk asked with a syrupy southern drawl.

"Yes," the woman answered. "I'd like to inquire about the purchase of a certain property."

"Do you have any paperwork?" the clerk asked.

"Yes."

The woman handed the clerk the survey papers.

"I think it's called Johnson's Farm."

The clerk tensed. She unrolled the survey documents then nodded.

"Yes, this is the property," she said.

"Excellent!" the woman took off her shades, revealing her dark brown eyes. "Do you know who I should speak to about purchasing the property?"

"The land belongs to the county," the woman said. "Although I'm not sure you would want to purchase it."

The woman's smile faded. "Is it for sale?"

"Yes."

"Then I wish to purchase it."

The clerk hesitated and the woman rolled her eyes. "This isn't about to get racial, is it?" she said. "Because if it is I am more than willing . . ."

The clerk shook her head. "No, no. It's not that. Claymont County is very progressive. It's just . . ."

"Just what?"

The clerk hesitated. She wasn't about to get tangled in a racial discrimination lawsuit over a haunted piece of property. Besides, whoever his woman was, she wasn't local. She wasn't worth the warning.

"Nothing, ma'am," the clerk said. "I apologize if I offended you."

"Apology accepted," the woman said with a smile. "My lawyer will be here in a week to handle the details. I hope the land will still be available."

"It will," the clerk said.

"Thank you so much," the woman replied. She turned with a flourish and strode out of the building, leaving a vacuum of style in her wake.

Her lawyer arrived a week later as she promised, and after eighty years the Johnson Farm had a new owner. The legal documents listed the woman's name as Naomi Sunshine. As was the nature of folks in Claymont County, the local folks tried to discover who was this woman and why did she come to the county. Some said she favored the Dawsons; others thought she might be related to that Rooks boy who played quarterback for Fox Valley State College then went to the pros. Whoever she was, Naomi came to Claymont County with a purpose. Not only did she buy the Johnson's property, she purchased the old Crowder land and the pine plantation that used to be Foley property. But the only property she developed was Johnson's Farm. Every company hired to do the work on the property was Black owned. If a local Black company wasn't available, a company was hired from out of town. The property was cleared, and a small home was constructed a few yards behind the original home. It was when renovations began on the original home that the locals took notice. Although most of the people who lived during those earlier dark days had gone on to Glory, the story of Johnson Farm lingered. Would some tragedy befall Miss Sunshine? Only time would tell.

Miss Sunshine's plans for the old house were revealed when she finally applied for a business permit. The house was to be transformed into a vegan restaurant, the first in the county. Most of the vegetables would be grown on the farm. Miss Sunshine hired local Black farmers to clear, plant and maintain the land. By the time Miss Sunshine returned she'd become a local celebrity. The restaurant opened with great fanfare and became an instant success. Sunshine, as the restaurant was named, became a favorite stop for the health-conscious road weary and the local vegan community. Naomi was the perfect hostess; although she didn't work in the restaurant, she would often stroll from her house to talk to customers or would be seen tending the fields or her garden. Local and state news channels clamored to interview this young, budding entrepreneur but she refused them all.

* * *

Fulton Albright, station owner of WTAQ TV, The Sound of the South, arrived at his office Monday morning and received a pleasant surprise. The mysterious Naomi Sunshine finally agreed to an interview! She requested Brandon Calhoun, which was a great choice.

21

Fulton assembled his crack team and sent them immediately to the restaurant. Naomi greeted them with her warm smile, leading the crew to a table near the busy kitchen. Brandon Calhoun, a straw blonde local boy, former football standout and Communications graduate from University of Georgia, flashed his perfect smile as he entered the establishment. When they reached the table, Brandon, being the southern gentleman that he was, pulled Naomi's chair out for her before sitting and checking his mike.

"Thank you for allowing us to interview you, Miss Sunshine," he said.

"It's my pleasure," Naomi replied.

"I must say you've accomplished so much in a short period of time."

"It's my nature," Naomi replied. "Once I set my mind on something, it gets done with a quickness."

Brandon laughed. "You've put Claymont County on the map. You could have built your restaurant anywhere. Why here?"

"I wanted to return to my roots," Naomi said.

Brandon's eyebrows rose. "Your roots?"

"Yes. I grew up in Atlanta, but my great grandmother was from Claymont."

"This is fascinating!" Brandon said. "My family had been here for generations. She may be someone I know."

"That's likely," Naomi replied. "My grandmother told me there were a few good white people in the county back in the day. Maybe your family was in that group."

"I would like to think so," Brandon said. "Thank goodness for progress."

"Indeed," Naomi replied.

A waiter came from the kitchen carrying a tray with two cups and a teapot.

"Ah," Brandon said. "Is this some of Miss Sunshine's famous organic tea?"

"Yes, it is," Naomi said.

"I've been dying to try it."

Naomi poured Brandon a cup and he took a sip.

"This is fantastic," he said.

"Thank you. It's a blend handed down from my great grandmother. The rumor is that she was a root worker."

Brandon sipped more tea before placing his cup down.

"Let's talk about that," Brandon said.

"Well, the family story is that my great grandmother came into some money then left the county and moved to Atlanta. She started a business selling home remedies. She was able to send my grandmother to school. She graduated from Spelman then moved to Washington D.C. My mother and I were born there."

"And your mother?"

"She graduated from Howard and became a doctor."

Brandon sipped more tea. "I guess the medical profession wasn't for you?"

"It wasn't my cup of tea," Naomi replied with smile.

"And the rest is history," Brandon said. "You know I have a link to this property as well. My great grandfather owned it briefly. Unfortunately, he took ill and died before he could develop it."

"You mean Bill Calhoun?"

Brandon's smile faded.

"Yes. That's him."

Naomi smiled. "I did my research, too. My great grandmother was known around here as Miss Hattie. Miss Hattie Johnson, to be exact. My grandmother was five when they left the county."

Brandon winced and rubbed his stomach.

"It seems this tea doesn't agree with me."

"Really? I'm surprised."

Brandon stood and wobbled.

"I think we're done here," he said. "It was interesting talking to you, Naomi."

"Miss Sunshine," Naomi corrected. "Before you go. I have something for you."

Brandon's eyebrows rose. "For me?"

"Well, not exactly."

Naomi reached behind the counter and picked up a pink envelope.

"Give this to your grandmother. She's still with us, isn't she?"

"Yes, she is. She lives in Tidwell County."

Naomi smiled. "That's nice. You make sure she gets that."

Brandon nodded. "I will."

The TV crew packed up their gear and left the restaurant. Naomi had Brandon's tea put in a to-go cup and the crew headed back to the station with the scoop of the year. Later that day Brandon drove out to Grandma Betty's house. Grandma Betty sat on the screened-in front porch as she always did in the afternoon, enjoying the sun and her azaleas. Brandon sauntered up to the porch, the pink envelope from Miss Sunshine in his hand.

She greeted her grandson with a hug and kiss.

"Grandma, I interviewed Naomi Sunshine today," Brandon said.

"That colored girl who owns the restaurant off the highway?" Grandma said.

Brandon frowned. "We don't call them colored anymore. Anyway, she told me to give you this."

Brandon handed his grandma the envelope. Betty opened it.

"I can't read this," she said. "Go get me my glasses."

Brandon entered the house and found grandma's reading glasses on the coffee table in the parlor. Betty put on her glasses and read the paper. It was a check written to her daddy, Billy Calhoun, for five thousand dollars. Included with the check was a note. Grandma read it.

"Oh . . ." she fainted.

Brandon shook his grandma back to consciousness.

"What's wrong?" he asked.

Grandma gave him the note.

"Hope you enjoyed the tea."
Miss Hattie

Bigger

Zeke jumped off the front porch of the shotgun shack, almost landing on the hound dog and scattering the chickens rooting around the persimmon tree. His back burned where Poppa's belt hit him. Zeke darted across the freshly plowed field and plunged into the pines, ignoring the briars cutting into his bare arms.

"Bring yo ass back here, boy!" Poppa shouted. "Running just gonna make it worse!'

Zeke didn't slow down. He wasn't going to let Poppa beat him anymore. He wasn't his real poppa anyway. His poppa . . . his real daddy . . . died working for the railroad five years ago. His daddy was a good church going man that treated him and Mama like Sunday morning. His daddy was a big, dark man with skin smooth as glass and a smile that shamed the sun.

Zeke ran across the dirt road, up the hill and down the other side to Little Uchee Creek. He waded across the muddy waterway and kept going until he reached Big Uchee Creek. There he finally halted, leaning against a big mulberry tree tilting over the bank. He gasped for breath, tears weaving down his cheeks.

"I wish I was bigger," he panted. He eased down, his legs dangling over the bank. "Mama wouldn't need no man. I could plow the field and chop the wood. I could feed the mule and the chickens."

The mulberry's bark was rough yet soothing against his back. He wished he had his cane pole and some worms. He could fish until Poppa wasn't drunk anymore. If he brought home a couple of bream or catfish everybody would be happy. Zeke closed his eyes.

"But if I was bigger..." he said, and did nothing till, warm with sun, he fell asleep.

* * *

They swarmed over the creek, buzzing before Zeke like an aggravated cloud and blinking like fireflies. But it was too early for fireflies. The swarm edged closer to the sleeping boy then engulfed him in a bright pulsing iridescence.

* * *

Zeke felt warmth on his eyelids and opened his eyes to rainbows. He shut them; shook his head hard and opened them again. The rainbows were gone. Instead, he looked up into a starry night sky.

He jerked up and bumped his head on a low hanging branch.

"Mama gonna whup me now!" he moaned. Zeke ran through the dark woods back to the house, careful to take his time wading through the creeks. He heard Mama calling him the closer he got to the house. She stood on the front porch holding a kerosene lamp as he stumbled into the yard.

"I'm sorry, Mama," he said. "I feel asleep under the mulberry tree by Big Uchee . . ."

Zeke stopped talking. Mama was looking at him, her mouth hanging open and her eyes as wide as saucers.

"Mama, you alright?"

Just then Poppa pushed open the screen door so hard it slammed against the wall.

"'Bout time you brought your no good behind back! Where . . . what the hell?"

Poppa's eyes got small like pinheads. Zeke looked back at them, wondering what was wrong.

"That boy done went and got him some hoodoo," Poppa said. He rolled up his sleeves, a mean grin coming to his face. "We'll, I ain't scared of no hoodoo," he said as he swaggered down the steps. "I'll whip his ass no matter how big he is."

Zeke scratched his head as Poppa stomped down the stairs, his fists balled up. What was he talking about? Then Poppa was standing right in his face, and he understood. He wasn't looking up at Poppa. He was looking *at* him.

Then a bright light blinded him, and his mouth started hurting real bad. He fell on his butt, tears welling up in his eyes. Poppa stood over him, rubbing his right fist with his other hand.

"I told you I wasn't worried about no hoodoo," he said.

Another light appeared over Zeke's head. Poppa's eyes looked like they were going to pop out of his head.

"What in the hell?"

The swarm that hovered over Zeke at the creek swirled down over him with its flashing colors. Zeke's mouth stopped hurting and he felt strong. The swarm lifted, bringing Zeke back to his feet.

"I ain't scared of you no more," he said. "I'm going to fight you!"

Poppa didn't say nothing. He staggered back, his mouth wide like a bass. Zeke was confused until he realized he wasn't looking *at* Poppa; he was looking down on him. Poppa got smaller as Zeke grew and grew until he could see the top of the house. It was then one of the swirling lights broke from the flight and landed on Zeke's nose. It wasn't a light, and it wasn't a bug. It was a little naked person with wings like a rainbow and curly hair on its head like him. It grinned at him, jumped off his nose and flew back into the swirl.

Zeke looked down and saw Poppa run into the house. He hunched low then watched Poppa scurry down the hallway to the back door. Zeke reached into the house, his hand barely fitting through the door. He grabbed Poppa by the leg and dragged him onto the porch. Once he got him outside, he wrapped his hand around him and stared him in the face.

"Who's gonna whup who?" Zeke said.

Poppa started shivering, and Zeke felt something warm in his hand.

"You peed on me!" he shouted. Zeke tossed Poppa into the trees and wiped his damp hand on his pants. He heard branches breaking as Poppa tumbled to the ground behind the house.

The little flying people swarmed around Zeke again. The roof came closer and closer until he couldn't see it anymore. He stood before the house, looking up at the front porch the way he always did. He wasn't big Zeke anymore. Mama crept up to him like a child trying to scare a cat.

"Baby, what you done got yourself into?" she said.

Zeke poked out his chest. "Nothing, mama. These little naked people made me big so I could beat up Poppa. Now we don't have to worry about him no more."

The little people danced around his head, and he danced with them until mama grabbed his shoulders and rushed him into the house, slamming the doors behind them. She dragged him to the bathroom, took off his dirty clothes and bathed him like she was trying to wash the hoodoo out of him.

"I'm alright Mama," Zeke said. "We alright!"

Mama dried him off, put on his sleeping clothes, and put him to bed.

"Good night, mama,' he whispered. Mama looked at him with love and fear in her eyes.

"Don't be scared," he said as he drifted to sleep. "We gonna be real good from now on."

Zeke and Mama got on alright, just like he said. They tended the farm on their own. Zeke discovered that he didn't need to be big to do most of the chores, but when he did, the naked flying people would show up and shine their colors on him. At first Mama would run in the house when they came, but gradually she would just sit and watch as they made Zeke bigger. One hot summer night Zeke and Mama rested on the front porch drinking tea. The hound dog slept by their feet and a cool breeze drifted through the pines from the creek. Fireflies flittered under the big red oak, the old tree's canopy thick with leaves. Just then the flying folks came in with the wind. They mixed in with the fireflies, dancing around the bugs.

"Them must be angels," Mama said. "Tiny angels sent to help us out."

Zeke never thought about that before.

"Daddy sent them," he said. "He knew we needed help, so he sent them from Heaven."

Mama wrapped her arms around him then pulled him tight.

"Maybe he did, Zeke. Maybe he did."

When harvest season come Mr. Calhoun sent his boys to mama's to help pick the vegetables like he'd done ever since Daddy passed away. When they rumbled up the dirt road in their Ford, they were surprised to see bushels lined up in front of the house, Zeke and Mama sitting on the porch with big smiles on their faces. Nathaniel Calhoun, the oldest and the biggest of the boys, jumped out the truck scratching his bald head.

"How in the world did y'all do that by yourself?"

"Don't worry about it," Mama said. "Y'all taking us to market or what?"

They rode up to Columbus and sold everything at the Farmer's Market. The Calhouns took Zeke and Mama to Woolworth's. Mama bought herself a yellow dress and hat, and then bought Zeke a brand-new suit.

"Why do I need a suit?" Zeke asked.

"Cause we going to church this Sunday," Mama said. "We gonna thank the Lord for his blessings."

The next day Mama and Zeke sat in the front pew in Little Bethel AME Zion Church. Everybody was happy to see them, the women telling Mama how pretty she looked and how glad they were she got rid of that no-good man, the men rubbing Zeke's head and telling him how much he looked like his daddy. Just around the time Reverend Williams told the ushers to take their seats there was a commotion at the back of the church. Zeke turned around to see a tall man in Army dress blues striding down the aisle, a big white smile on his cocoa face as bright as the medals on his chest. He sat right beside Mama and nodded.

"How you doing, ma'am?" he said. His voice was deep like a borrow pit. Mama's eyelids fluttered.

"I'm fine, suh" she answered. "How are you?"

Zeke didn't think the man's smile could get any brighter, but it did.

"Just fine, ma'am. Just fine."

The army man looked at Zeke and smiled. "How you doing, son?"

Zeke couldn't help but smile back. He liked the way the army man called him son.

"I'm fine, suh," he answered.

Mama and the army man talked for a long time after church. Zeke knew mama liked him. She was looking at him like she used to look at Daddy and Poppa. He seemed to be okay. For a minute Zeke got nervous but then he went to play with the other boys. He wasn't going to worry, because if anything went wrong between Mama and the army man, Zeke could always get... bigger.

Lady in the Lake

Coot pushed the johnboat into the lake. He looked back at Diane with a frown.

"You coming?"

Diane bit her lip as she twisted her braid.

"I don't know about this," she said.

"You gotta come now," he said. "I'm gonna get an ass whupping when daddy finds out I took his boat. I ain't getting one for nothing."

Diane looked left to right like somebody was watching.

"You sure they gonna be there?"

"Been there every day so far. Ain't no reason for them not to be there today."

"You ain't just telling me this to get me in the boat with you, are you?"

"Shoot girl! I ain't studdin' you like that. We friends."

Diane knew that. Coot was like a brother. She was just looking for an excuse to say no.

"Come on now, girl!" Coot said.

Diane sighed. She rolled up her jeans to her knees and climbed into the johnboat. It wasn't that she was scared of the water. She loved it. She went swimming at the Sand Hills rec center almost every day during the summer. Sometimes she would sneak down to the lake with her swimsuit and swim. She loved the lake water better. It was natural and alive, touching her skin as if she belonged there. Sometimes Coot would swim with her, but not long. He was always scared a water moccasin or snapping turtle would bite him. But she wasn't afraid.

Diane grabbed a paddle and they rowed together to the middle of the lake.

"What you doing way out here?" she asked Coot.

"Bass don't bite out here."

"Catfish do," Coot said. "At least the big ones."

"You don't like catfish," Diane said.

"Damn sure don't," Coot said. "But grandma do."
Coot reached into his pocket and pulled out a handful
of dark purple round objects.

"Them muscadines?" Diane asked.

Coot nodded.

"Give me some!"

"Un uh. This is for the lake people."
Diane's eyes went wide. "They like muscadines?"

"Sh'oll do," Coot said. "Watch."

"Can I have at least one?"
Coot looked at Diane and grinned. He handed her two
then popped one in his mouth before dropping another
one into the water.

"Come see!" he said.
Diane and Coot watched the muscadine swirl down-
ward. Diane gripped the side of the johnboat while she
chewed the pungent, sweet fruit.

"Ain't nothing happening," she said.

"Just wait. It's almost deep enough," Coot said.
The wild grape was almost invisible when a hand
reached out and grabbed it.

Diane sat straight up, her mouth so wide the half
chewed muscadine fell out into the boat. Coot smiled tri-
umphantly.

"Told you," he said.

"Give me another one!" Diane said.
Coot dropped the muscadine into her palm. Diane
tossed it over the side then waited. This time the grape
was only halfway down before the hand appeared. Long
elegant fingers clasped the muscadine between them, the
body of the being holding it obscured by the murky

water. Then something happened neither Coot nor Diane expected. The hand began rising toward them.

"Shoot!" Coot exclaimed.

Diane and Coot grabbed their paddles and rowed as fast as they could. Diane dared to look back and saw the hand holding the muscadine come to the surface, the thin arm cutting a wake as it rapidly closed on them.

"Paddle faster!" she yelled.

The johnboat jerked to a stop. Diane yelped and kept paddling, but the boat didn't move. She jerked her head around. Two hands gripped the back of the boat; the muscadine lay inside the boat. A head rose over the back of the boat and Diane gasped. A woman stared at her; her beautiful brown face lit with a smile.

"Move!" Coot shouted.

He shoved Diane aside, shuffling on his knees with his paddle raised over his head.

"Imma bust your head wide . . ."

The woman's eyes went wide then she disappeared below the water. Coot turned to Diane, his expression a mesh of fear and wonder.

"What in the whole wide world . . ."

The johnboat flipped over, dumping them in the lake.

Diane panicked for a moment, her arms flailing. She calmed down after a minute, opening her eyes and searching for the shore. Coot treaded water not far away.

"We got to turn the boat over," he said.

"Naw, we got to git," Diane said.

"Daddy's gonna whup me if I don't come back with his boat!"

"And how we gone get it back?" Diane said "We ain't got no paddles."

Diane swam for the bank.

"You ain't gonna help me?" Coot complained.

"I'm getting out this lake as fast as I can," Diane said. "Come on!"

Coot whined then swam with Diane toward the bank. They were halfway there when something grabbed Diane's ankle. She shook her leg, thinking it might have hung up on a sunken tree. But then whatever it was jerked her leg so hard she yelped in pain. Coot stopped swimming. He treaded water as he turned around.

"Diane, what's . . ."

Diane's ears flooded with water as she was dragged down. She tried hard to kick her leg free, but the grip held tight. Diane held her breath before looking down. The lake lady gazed at her, a smile on her face as she pulled Diane deeper.

She's killing me and smiling!

The lake lady finally stopped dragging her into the lake's depth. She grabbed Diane's arms, pushing them to her sides. With gentle eyes her smile faded.

"Open your mouth."

The voice rang in Diane's head. Diane shook her head.

"I'll drown if I do."

The woman's face became stern.

"You'll die if you don't."

Diane had no choice. She couldn't hold her breath any longer, and the lake lady wasn't going to let her go. She opened her mouth and the water rushed in, choking her. Diane fought to swim but the woman held her still. She choked, then coughed, but she did not drown. After a time, her breathing became normal.

"How am I'm doing this?"

The lake lady answered with a grin. She took Diane's hand.

"Come with me. I have something to show you."

Diane and the lake lady swam deeper. Bluegills and bass scattered as they neared until they reached a gaping hole at the lake bottom. Warm water escaped from the opening. The lake lady tugged at her hand then pointed at the hole.

"We going in there?"

The lake lady nodded. *"Don't be afraid. This is the best part."*

They entered. What appeared as a hole was a pitch-black tunnel. Diane's fear was abated by the lady's firm but reassuring grip on her wrist. They swam until a faint light appeared before them, growing larger with each stroke. The tunnel expanded into a large cave that teemed with people that looked just like the lake lady.

"Where did y'all come from?"

"Africa, just like you," the lake lady replied. *"When our folks escaped from the plantations, some went south, some went north, and some came here."*

"But how?"

The lake lady smiled. *"That's a question for another time."*

Diane watched the lake people swim to and fro. It was just like her town, but underwater.

The lake lady tugged her wrist.

"Time for you to go back," she said. *"Your people are probably looking for you."*

The lake lady led Diane back to the lake. They floated together, Diane moving her legs, the lake lady waving her tail.

"Why did you show me this?" Diane asked.

"Because someone above needs to know," the lady replied.

"Why me?"

The lady smiled. *"You'll find out. Now go."*

Diane began swimming, then stopped.

"My name is Diane," she said. *"What's yours?"*
"What do you want it to be?" the lake lady asked.
"Angela," Diane said.
"Then I am Angela to you."
Diane smiled then waved.
"Bye, Angela!"
"Goodbye, Diane."
Diane swam for the surface. When her head breached the water, she coughed hard until the water was gone from her lungs.
"There she is!"
Diane turned to her left. Coot high-stepped through the shallows then dove into the water. Diane's mama was right behind him. Daddy and some of their neighbors remained on the bank, hugging and thanking the Lord. Mama out swam Coot, reaching her first. She hugged her tight.
"Baby!" she said. "Coot said you drowned! I knew he was lying. My baby swims like a bream!"
Diane squeezed mama back. "Mama, I got to tell you what happened!"
"Not now baby. Let's get you out of this water."
Diane and mama swam toward the shore, Diane looking back now and then hoping to see Angela.
"What you looking at, baby?" Mama asked. "Did you lose something?"
"No," Diane said.
They reached Coot. He swam to Diane, his cheeks streaked with tears.
"I'm sorry I left you!" he said. "I couldn't find you."
"It's okay," Diane managed to say. "I'm fine."
Daddy stood up to his waist in the lake as they neared the shore. He scooped Diane up into his arms like a baby.
"You alright?"

"Yes, sir."

"Everybody can go home now," he shouted to the spectators. "Everything is fine."

"You should take her to the hospital," Oscar Silas said. He leaned on his cane, sharing his ever-present scowl.

"Ain't nobody got money for that," Daddy replied. "My girl is fine. Y'all go on home."

They walked to the pickup truck.

"Coot, you ride in the cab with Joe," mama said. "Me and Diane riding in the bed."

"You sure about that, Beatrice?" Daddy asked.

"I'm sure," mama said. "We can dry off a little bit."

"Alright," Daddy said. "Come on, boy."

Daddy and Coot climbed into the cabin. The truck rumbled to life, and they bounced down the dirt road toward the street. Mama hugged Diane.

"Now what is it you had to tell me?"

"There's a lady in the lake!" Diane blurted. "She pulled me down into the water and I found out I can breathe it! Then she took me to a cave where there was a whole lot of people just like her!"

"So, she finally decided to introduce herself," mama said.

Diane jumped then pulled away from mama.

"You know her?"

"Yes, I do," mama said. "Every girl in our family comes to meet her sooner or later."

"So, you can breathe water, too?"

Mama chuckled. "I used to be able to. Then I got married and had you and forgot about the water. But I knew you were next. First time we brought you to the lake you tried to jump in. Your daddy like to had a fit. We had to fight you to get you back to the car."

"I don't understand," Diane said.

39

"Well, it's time you did," mama said. "Did she ask you to give her a name?"

"Yes! I named her Angela."

Mama smiled.

"I named her Mary."

"What's her real name?" Diane asked.

Mama hugged Diane and she hugged mama back.

"I'll tell you that and a lot more once we get home. Okay?"

Diane smiled. "Okay!"

Diane glanced over her shoulder at the lake as it diminished in the distance. She knew she would return, and she knew she would see the lady in the lake again.

Down South

Roscoe Hill removed his chauffeur hat as he entered Miss Liza's mansion, patting his hair in place with his free hand. Although he worked for Miss Liza for almost 10 years, he'd never set foot inside the expansive home on East 127th Street, Harlem. Whatever she summoned him for had to be special.

Celia, Miss Liza's elderly maid, led him into the antique-laden foyer then through the gauntlet of oil portraits hanging on the hallway walls leading to the parlor. Miss Liza sat alone, her ecru skin and light green house dress illuminated by the sunlight reflecting from the large picture mirror opposite the window. She took a sip of tea then placed the gold inlaid teacup on the matching saucer on the table before her. Her eyes fell on Roscoe, and she smiled.

"That will be all, Celia," she said.

"I'll be right outside if you need me," Celia said as she cast a distrustful glance at Roscoe.

"There's no need for that," Miss Liza replied. "Roscoe drives me every day. If I can't trust him, I can't trust anyone."

Celia glared at Roscoe.

"You behave yourself, boy," she whispered.

Roscoe glared back. "Mind your own business, you old biddy."

He smiled as he turned his attention to Miss Liza.

"You asked for me, ma'am?" he said.

"Yes, I did, Roscoe. Have a seat."

Roscoe sat in the chair next to the door.

Miss Liza turned toward him. "How long have you worked for me, Roscoe?"

"Ten years come this May," he said.

Miss Liza laughed. "You've outlasted all my husbands."

Roscoe lowered his head, hiding his grin.

"I reckon so, ma'am."

"Aren't you from down South?"

"Yes ma'am."

"Where?" she asked.

"Alabama, ma'am. A little place called Seale."

"I've never heard of it," she said. "My parents are from the South, Atlanta to be exact. But you know that."

"Yes, I do, ma'am."

"You fought in the war too, didn't you Roscoe?"

Roscoe tensed. "Yes, I did, ma'am. I was a Hellfighter."

Miss Liza knew about his time in the army. He fought at Champagne-Marne and Meuse-Argonne, earning the Croix de Guerre medal from the French. Roscoe came home thinking the medal and his time served would make a difference, but it didn't. The Klan almost lynched him outside of Phenix City, Alabama, so he got out the South as soon as he could. If he'd had the money, he would have gone back to France. Instead, he ended up a taxi driver in New York, where he met Miss Liza. She was so impressed by his manners she hired him as her personal chauffeur.

"Miss Liza, excuse me for being direct, but why did you ask me here?"

Miss Liza's smile faded. "Roscoe, I need you to pick up a package for me, a very special package."

"That ain't no problem, ma'am," he said, somewhat relieved. "Where do I need to go? Brooklyn? Manhattan?"

Miss Liza looked at him square in the eyes. "Savannah, Georgia."

Roscoe shook his head. "I don't think..."

"Listen to me, Roscoe," she said. "You're the only person I can trust to do this. You're from the South so you know to behave down there. If I sent one of my New York men they'd be lynched before sunset. You're an ex-soldier so you can handle yourself. I'll pay you one thousand dollars up front and one thousand dollars when you return with the package, plus expenses."

Two thousand dollars would set Roscoe straight for quite some time. But he knew his answer long before Miss Liza began her persuading talk.

"I'm sorry, Miss Liza," Roscoe said. "I can't do it."

"Roscoe, please," Miss Liza said. "This is very important to me."

Roscoe stood then put on his hat. "The last thing I want to do is disappoint you ma'am. You've been good to me. But this is one thing I can't do."

"Roscoe…" Miss Liza said.

Roscoe backed out the room.

"I'm sorry, ma'am. I'm sorry."

Roscoe turned then walked away.

"Roscoe, wait!"

Roscoe kept walking. Celia waited at the door, a grin on her face.

"You done messed up now, boy," she said. "Ain't no way Miss Liza going to keep you on now. Good riddance to bad rubbish, I say."

Roscoe pushed by the maid then continued to the garage. He trudged up the stairs to his room. Celia was right. He would have to leave and find another job. He was fond of Miss Liza; she reminded him of the daughter he never had. But there were some things he just couldn't do. Going back down South was one of them.

He opened his closet then dragged out his trunk, the same trunk he was issued when he enlisted. He opened it and was engulfed in memories. He gazed upon his

43

uniform, neatly folded and pressed; the Croix de Guerre still pinned to the pocket. Atop the uniform was his bolo knife in its army issue canvas sheath. He picked up the weapon then pulled it free, studying the long, razor-edged blade. The last time he held it in his hand was in Phenix City, Alabama. It was the only thing that stood between him and a lynch mob. He closed his eyes then shook the memories from his head. A man who fought for his country shouldn't be treated that way. He had the right to defend himself.

He sheathed the knife, then placed it back into the trunk. Roscoe shuffled over to his dresser, opened the drawers then began removing his clothes and placing them neatly into the trunk.

"And where do you think you're going?"

Roscoe turned to see Miss Liza standing in his doorway.

"Well, Miss Liza, I figured since I turned down your request, you'd be ready to fire me."

Miss Liza sat in his desk chair. "You figured wrong. You're like family, Roscoe, and Lord knows I don't have much of that."

Roscoe sat on the foot of his bed. "I appreciate you thinking of me that way. But I don't..."

Miss Liza grabbed his hand.

"Listen to me, Roscoe. I'm going to tell you the whole story. After I'm done, if you tell me you won't do it, I'll never bother you again."

"I'm listening," Roscoe answered.

Miss Liza swallowed. "When I was 15, I got pregnant. The father was a white boy, Leonard Shuman."

Roscoe leaned back stunned, almost pulling Miss Liza from her seat.

"Pregnant? By a white boy?" Roscoe felt anger rising inside. His grip on Miss Liza's hand tightened.

"It's not what you think, Roscoe," Miss Liza said quickly. "Leonard and I loved each other. Leonard's parents were prominent in New York politics, just like my parents. But Leonard's parents weren't about to let their son marry a colored girl, and my parents weren't about to let me throw my life away on some weak-minded white boy. We fought them, but in the end our parents won. Leonard's parents sent him to Europe; my parents sent me to Atlanta where I lived until I gave birth. They took my baby from me, and then put her up for adoption."

Miss Liza's eyes glistened. Roscoe took a handkerchief from his drawer then handed it to her.

"I held her in my arms, Roscoe. She was so beautiful. I made a promise that day that I would find her, no matter where they took her. Five years ago, I did."

"In Savannah?" Roscoe asked. Miss Liza nodded.

"It took a long time and a lot of money, but I found her living with foster parents. I sent them a letter explaining who I was and what I wanted to do. I promised I would not try to take her from them. I only wanted to communicate with her. They agreed."

"So, you ready to break your promise now," Roscoe said.

"About three months ago my letters started coming back. I've been going crazy ever since. I think she's still in Savannah, but for some reason her family decided to stop corresponding."

Miss Liza opened her purse, reached inside, then took out a picture. She handed the picture to Roscoe.

"Her name is Mary Ann," Miss Liza said.

"She looks just like you," Roscoe said.

"I want my baby, Roscoe. I want my baby home. I'll pay you whatever you want. Please do this for me. Please."

Miss Liza bent over then cried into her hands. Roscoe leaned toward her, placing a gentle hand on her shoulder.

"I'll do it," he said. "I'll go get your baby, Miss Liza."

Miss Liza lunged toward him, wrapping her arms around him.

"Thank you, Roscoe. Thank you!"

Roscoe held her, stroking her hair. He imagined his own daughter asking him the same question. There would be no doubt he would do it, even if it meant returning to the South and risking his life again.

"It'll be alright, Miss Liza. It'll be alright," he said.

* * *

Roscoe took the subway to the train station. He paid for his ticket then took a seat in the cabin. Once they crossed the Mason-Dixon Line he'd have to move to the colored section, but for now he sat where he chose. The train left promptly; Roscoe settled into his seat then quickly fell to sleep, lulled by the rocking rhythm of the train. He dreamed of the day he discovered what he was. He was twelve. There was a storm that day, the worst storm he'd ever seen. He, mama, and daddy crouched in the kitchen under the table, mama praying like a preacher on revival Sunday. They heard a loud crack then everything went black. When he woke, they were still under the table, except the large white oak that grew beside the house was on top of them. Daddy was still, but mama moaned and prayed. Roscoe pushed against the tree, straining with all his might, but it was too heavy. He cried out for help until he was hoarse, but no one answered. In a fit of rage, he pushed against the tree again and it shifted. Roscoe kept pushing until they were free. He picked up Daddy and took him outside, and then he returned for mama. She looked at him with wonder.

"God done sent us an angel," she said. "An angel!"

Weeks later, after the excitement and tragedy of the storm had passed, Daddy and Mama called him to their room.

"The Lord done gave you a gift, boy," Daddy said. "And it ain't one to be trifling with."

"You have to keep it secret, unless other folks find out and try to get you to do bad things with it," Mama said. "It's bad enough being colored in this world. What you have will only make it worse."

"But I can help people!" he said.

"Listen up boy!" Daddy said. "You promise you won't tell nobody. You hear?"

"Yes, sir," Roscoe said.

Mama got up and went into the bedroom. She returned with her worn leather King James Bible

"Swear to God," Mama said.

Roscoe placed a trembling hand on Mama's Bible.

"I swear I won't use my strength or let anyone know," he said.

Mama smiled then kissed his forehead.

Roscoe jumped awake. He halfway expected to see Seale, Alabama. He settled into his seat. It was hard, but he kept that promise for most of his life. It wasn't until the war did he use his powers again. That was another nightmare.

The train eased into the Savannah station in the afternoon in the midst of a hot humid day. Roscoe peered out the window, his stomach churning with emotions. During the journey down he'd spent his time lending a hand to the porters, chatting with the black men who served the passengers and kept the train running smoothly. Most were from the south like him, fleeing Jim Crow or seeking a better life in the North. From the conversation nothing much had changed. One conversation with the men warned him to keep on his guard, even though the men didn't realize the warning in their words. They were playing Spades when it began.

Moses Jones, a tall light-skinned man with slick-backed hair dropped a seven of diamonds on the table.

"You fight in the war?" he asked Roscoe.

Roscoe nodded. "Yeah. I was there, but I wouldn't call it fighting," he lied.

Mike Stevens, a thick muscled man with skin like onyx and glittering white teeth, flashed an easy smile as he cut Moses' seven with a three of spades.

"I think I dug more holes in France than I did in Arkansas," he said.

Pepper Lewis, another light-skinned man with freckled cheeks, cursed as he dropped a two of hearts.

"Them boys from the 369th gave them hell, though," he said. "A few of them won medals from the French. You meet any of them, Roscoe?"

Roscoe ended the hand when he dropped an eight of spades and everyone moaned.

"No," he said. "I heard they were something else."

"Sho' were," Mike said. "Gave them Huns hell."

"Shoulda stayed in France," Pepper said. "You heard about that one that got lynched in Alabama?"

Everyone but Roscoe shook their heads. Roscoe picked up the cards and shuffled them for the next game.

"They say he was coming home, and a bunch of Klansmen met him getting off the train in Phenix City, Alabama. Dragged him back in the woods and lynched him."

"That's a damn shame," Moses said. "A goddamn shame."

"You ain't heard the rest of it, though," Pepper said. "Story is every last one of them Klansmen showed up dead. Every last one of them."

Mike folded his arms across his chest. "You a damn liar."

"Kiss my ass, Mike," Pepper said. "I ain't never lied. Some say it was that soldier boy's ghost."

Roscoe quit shuffling the cards, the memory of that night paralyzing him.

"Hey boy, you gonna deal them cards?" Pepper said.

Roscoe placed the deck on the table.

"Got to go," he said. "My stop's coming up."

Pepper laughed. "That story scared you, didn't it?"

Roscoe peered over his shoulder. "Something like that."

As Roscoe trudged back to his cabin, the images of that day in the Argonne Forest filled his head. The French officer sent him and Thaddeus Jones out to scout the trenches north of their position. Thaddeus was always a joker, making fun of everything and everyone. They laughed as they walked the narrow, filthy gully, Roscoe taking point. As they rounded a sharp turn in the trench, they came face to face with a column of Germans reoccupying the abandoned ditch. The Germans fired; Roscoe heard Thaddeus grunt then fall into the mud. Bullets struck Roscoe in the back as he tried to run, spinning him around. He dropped to his knees as more rounds battered his chest. But he didn't die. Roscoe shot back, emptying his Berthier rifle, then throwing it aside for his .32 Ruby. Germans fell before him, replaced by more as they came closer and closer. When his Ruby was empty, he snatched his U.S. issued bolo knife from his waist then charged, a rebel yell escaping his lips. The rest of the fight was close quarter carnage, Roscoe hacking and slashing like a madman. The Germans finally had enough of the black devil that would not die. They fled the trench, leaving Roscoe alone with his dying friend. When the rest of his unit reached them, he cradled Thaddeus's head in his arms, the wounds that hadn't healed still bleeding. In the medical tent they marveled at his recovery; if anyone thought it was unusual, they didn't say. Weeks later he was awarded the Croix de Guerre amidst the protests of the American Expeditionary Force commanders. A colored man didn't deserve such an honor. The French thought different.

* * *

Roscoe shook away the memory. He went back to his seat and gathered his things. The porters had been good company on the way down, but it was time to get serious. He waited until he was off the train before opening the leather pouch Miss Liza gave him before the trip. Inside was the address of her daughter's last known residence and a map with directions. Roscoe ventured into the historic city, falling into old habits drummed into him since he was a boy. He kept his head down, making sure not to make eye contact with any white folks, especially white women. He was a man of average height, so physically he didn't draw any attention. He deliberately wore his clothes two sizes too big. Most people saw him as overweight; in truth Roscoe was nearly three hundred pounds of hard muscle on a 5'8-inch frame.

He hesitated as he came within a few blocks of his destination. This was a neighborhood for rich white folks. There was no way he could enter without being noticed. What would a colored girl be doing in this kind of neighborhood, he thought. He shrugged, Miss Liza was light-skinned, and with her daughter being half white she could probably pass. Roscoe checked the directions one last time.

"Yeah, this is it," he said. "Lord help me."

He continued down the manicured street until he reached the address.

"Hey, boy! Where the hell you think you're going?"

Roscoe jumped then turned around to see the policeman standing on the sidewalk, his billy club in his hand. He was a lanky white man with straw blonde hair and a snarl.

"I'm sorry, sir, but I was told the people living here were looking for a gardener," Roscoe said.

"They might be, but you know damn well you ain't supposed to be on this walkway. Git on around back!"

Roscoe silently cursed himself. He shuffled down the walkway toward the officer.

"You better be glad I'm in a good mood today, boy," the officer said. "Otherwise, I'd take you downtown."

"Much obliged to you, sir," Roscoe said.

"Git on now before I change my mind," the officer said.

"Yes, sir," Roscoe replied. "Yes, sir."

Roscoe walked across the grass then worked his way up the side of the house to the rear entrance, all the while clenching and unclenching his fists. By the time he reached the back of the home he was trembling with anger.

"What you doing back here?" a husky female voice asked.

Roscoe looked up to see a dark brown woman dressed in a sky-blue maid uniform hanging clothes. A pleasant smile warmed her face despite her tone.

"I came back here to wait on the owners," he said. "I'm looking for yard work."

"Well, you a day late and a dollar short," the woman said.

Roscoe ambled to the fence.

"What do you mean by that?"

"The Finches moved out two weeks ago," she said. "Flew out of here like they owed somebody money. But that ain't so, because they got old money."

"My name is Roscoe Hill," Roscoe said.

"Lucinda Jones," the woman said. "Nice to meet you. Where you from?"

"New York," Roscoe said.

Lucinda laughed. "If you from New York I'm the Queen of England. You sound like you from right around here. Why you trying to be uppity?"

Roscoe laughed. "I'm originally from Alabama."

Lucinda smirked. "I thought so."

Lucinda walked back to the clothesline and began hanging the wash.

"Were they expecting you?"

"Apparently so," Roscoe whispered.

"What?"

"I said I guess not. My boss man said they'd be here."

"Looks like your boss man was wrong," Lucinda said.

"You got any idea where they went?" Roscoe asked.

"I don't, but Miss Henderson might. I'll ask her."

Lucinda went into the house. Roscoe waited for her return. He wondered if the Finches knew he was coming and ran off. But why would they do that? And who would have told them? The who popped in his head an instant later and he spat.

"That old biddy," he said.

Lucinda came back a few minutes later.

"Miss Henderson don't know nothing," Lucinda said.

"Thank you for asking," Roscoe replied.

"Hey, you got somewhere to stay?" Lucinda asked.

Roscoe pushed back his hat. "No."

"There's a place called Lulabelle's down by the marsh," Lucinda said. "It's a juke joint, but they have a couple of rooms upstairs they rent out. It's loud but the food is great and it's far enough out of town so no white folks will bother you. Now come over here and help me hang up these clothes. The sooner I'm done, the sooner I can leave."

"Your boss won't mind?"

"Hell naw," Lucinda said. "As long as she ain't got to pay you she's fine. She'll probably think you some old buck sweet on me."

Roscoe grinned as he made his way next door. Lucinda wasn't a bad looking woman, but she was way too young for him. Besides, he was in Savannah on business. He helped her hang the rest of the laundry then went out front to wait for her. She came from around back, a wide smile on her face.

"Give me your arm," she said.

Roscoe extended his arm and Lucinda wrapped hers around it.

"Now we're sweethearts until Miss Henderson can't see us no more."

Roscoe glanced at the house. The curtain was pulled aside; a white woman with a blonde bun on top of her head glared at them.

They strolled down the road until they were far from the house and into the city. Lucinda let go of Roscoe's arm. The two strolled to Black Savannah, a section of town that was in complete contrast to the newer section north and south of the city. Though the boll weevil destroyed the cotton crops, Savannah still thrived on shipping naval stores. The city had grown because of the prosperity, but like most cities that prosperity barely touched Negroes.

Lucinda walked up to a grocery store then began walking inside.

"I thought we were going to Lulabelle's," Roscoe said.

"We are. I got to pick up a few things before I go home."

"I need to get something too," Roscoe said.

They entered the grocery store. Lucinda strolled about the little store picking up items here and there; Roscoe went straight to the tool barrel. He searched through the hardware until he found a sturdy long handled shovel. When he met Lucinda at the counter her eyes went wide.

"Now what in the devil's name do you need that for?"

"I'm a yard man," Roscoe said. "It always helps to have a good shovel."

Roscoe and Lucinda paid for their goods then walked down the street until they reached the edge of the colored district.

"This is as far as I go," Lucinda said. "Keep going that way. You'll smell the marsh before you see it. Lulabelle's won't be far after that. Once you get inside ask for Slow Tom. He owns the place."

"Slow Tom?"

Lucinda laughed. "We call him that because he's the smartest man in Savannah. Come to think of it, he might be able to help you. Slow Tom knows everybody's business, colored or white."

"Thank you, Lucinda."

"You'll thank me by buying me dinner once you finish your business."

Roscoe looked puzzled. "My business?"

Lucinda tilted her head. "You mighta fooled them white folks, but you ain't fooled me. I know you ain't no yard man. I don't know what business you got with the

Finches, and I don't want to know. All I can say is be careful. This ain't New York."

"I'll be getting on then," Roscoe said.

By the time Roscoe reached the marsh the moon had risen over the humid night. The light wavered on the high tide; the air heavy with the wetland organic aroma. The sound of raucous laughter spurred on by a teasing melody of guitar and piano drifted toward him as he neared Lulabelle's. The large barn-like structure sat on a piece of land jutting into the marsh, surrounded by ancient live oaks heavy with Spanish moss. A tall man in coveralls leaned against a pickup truck, cradling a double-barreled shotgun in his thick arms. The man stood up straight as Roscoe approached.

"Who that is?" the man said in a thin, high-pitched voice.

Roscoe walked into the light with his hands raised.

"Roscoe Jones," he said. "Miss Lucinda told me I could find a place to stay the night here."

The man motioned Roscoe forward with the shotgun.

"Where you from?" he asked.

"Alabama, by way of New York."

The man smiled. "I'm Percy Green. My niece Corliss lives in New York. You know a girl named Corliss Lewis?"

"Can't say I do. New York is a big place."

"Yeah, but all the colored folks live in Harlem," the man said. "You sure you don't know her? Tall, yellow gal with big teeth."

"No, I don't know her."

The doorman shrugged. "Go on in. Slow Tom will be behind the bar. Can't miss him. He'll fix you up with a room if he has any."

Roscoe nodded then went inside. The blues band was playing a moody, sensual tune, the dancers slow dragging to the beat, grasping and grinding. Roscoe made his way across the packed floor toward a wide man with a bald head, a cigar protruding from the side of his mouth. His thick hands worked on a large beer mug as he rocked to the music.

"You Slow Tom?" Roscoe asked.

The man looked at Roscoe and his eyes narrowed, his white beard and eyebrows highlighted by his dark brown skin. He took the toothpick from his mouth and flicked it behind the counter.

"Who's asking?"

"Roscoe Hill," Roscoe said. "Miss Lucinda told me you rent rooms to colored folks."

Slow Tom placed the mug on the bar then extended his right hand. They shook, Slow Tom trying to crush Roscoe's hand with his grip. He yelped as Roscoe returned the favor. When he finally let go Tom jerked his hand away as if he'd touched fire.

"Damn, boy! Where'd you get a grip like that?"

"Grew up on a farm," Roscoe replied.

Tom flexed his hand.

"Rooms are a dollar a night. Might as well stay up until I close. Won't get much sleep with this going on. You play poker?"

"No, sir," Roscoe replied.

"Quit with that sir stuff. Just call me Tom."

Roscoe reached into his pocket then handed Tom a dollar.

"Now that's the kind of boarder I like!" Tom said. "Man pays up front. You hungry?"

"Yes, I am," Roscoe replied.

"I'll fix you up. Sit on down. I'll have Hattie mix you up a bucket."

"Hattie? Who's Lulabelle?"

Slow Tom laughed. "Ain't no Lulabelle. I just like the name."

He pushed open the swing door behind him.

"Hey, Hattie! Fix up a bucket! I got paying folks out here!"

Roscoe took a seat at the bar just as the music tempo picked up. Some of the couples reluctantly let go of each other, others took their business outside. Tom dropped a mason jar in front of Roscoe and grinned.

"Good stuff," he said. "Made it myself."

Roscoe picked up the jar then took a swig. It was good moonshine, stronger and smoother than most. He would need some liquid encouragement for what he was about to do.

"This is good," Roscoe said. "How much?"

"First one is on the house."

Roscoe finished the glass then wiped his mouth with his sleeve.

"Hey, Tom, you know anything about a white family called Finch?"

"I don't," Tom said. "But their maid Alvenia does. She came in here mad as hellfire. Said the Finches let her go without even a warning. Said they were moving."

"When did that happen?"

"About three weeks ago. She said they got a visit from some man from overseas, England, I think. She said he paid them a lot a money to give him that girl they'd been raising."

Roscoe's eyes went wide. "What happened to the man and the girl? Did they leave?"

"Not yet," Slow Tom said. "They're in a house nearby."

"Any idea where that house is?" Roscoe asked.

The kitchen door swung wide and Hattie came out with a steaming bucket, a wash towel wrapped around the metal wire handle. She dropped the bucket between Tom and Roscoe. Her eyes lingered on Roscoe as a grin came to her face.

"You gonna have to teach that boy how to eat crabs," she said. "He ain't from around here."

Tom took a crab out the bucket then instructed Roscoe the proper way to crack it.

"Why you trying to find them white folks?" Tom asked.

"I have a special delivery for them," he said. "My boss man told me to give it directly to them, nobody else."

"He picked a colored man for the job?"

"My boss man is colored."

Tom sucked the meat out of a crab leg.

"They're out at the old Wallace Plantation about five miles down the road. But you better have business with them. They got some local rednecks standing guard. You might mess around and get lynched."

"I'll be alright," Roscoe said. "That's been tried before. Didn't work out too well for them."

Tom began to laugh until he saw Roscoe's serious face. He leaned in close to Roscoe.

"Do me a favor; when you get caught, don't mention my name. I gots to live here."

Roscoe nodded while working on his third crab.

"I won't."

The men finished their meal as the band slowed down the music again for another round of slow dragging. Roscoe laid twenty-five cents on the counter for the meal, but Tom waved him off.

"You don't make a man pay for his last meal," he said.

Roscoe picked up his coin.

"You think your man Percy can take me close?"

Tom laughed. "You give him a dollar and he'll take you to the moon."

"Much obliged," Roscoe said.

He tipped his hat then went outside. Percy leaned against the pickup truck, whistling.

"Hey, Percy, Slow Tom says you'll take me anywhere I want to go for a dollar."

"Hell yeah!" Percy replied.

Roscoe handed Percy a dollar bill.

"I'll give you another if you wait for me," Roscoe said.

"It's a deal. Where we going?"

"Wallace Plantation," Roscoe said.

Percy hopped into the truck.

"Let's go!"

They followed a dirt road that took them deeper into the marsh. After a few miles Percy stopped the truck.

"This is as far as I go," he said.

Roscoe climbed out the truck then took his shovel from the bed.

"I'll be back," he said. "Wait here."

He trotted down the narrow road through a gauntlet of live oaks. A few minutes later a large house came into view. Roscoe counted six men in the front, four standing guard near the gate and two on the porch with rifles or shotguns. Roscoe slowed to a saunter as he walked into view.

"Who's there?" one of the men shouted. Roscoe didn't answer.

"God damn it, who is it?" the man said again.

Two of the guards approached him, their guns still cradled under their arms.

"Boy, what the hell are you doing out here this time…"

Roscoe smashed the man in the face with the shovel. He knocked the gun from the other guard's hand, then reached behind his back for the knife. As soon as his hand touched the hilt he was back in Alabama, surrounded by the sights and sounds of that horrible night. He cut the guard across his throat then sprinted for the house.

He heard a rifle report then flinched as a bullet struck his shoulder. He gritted his teeth, and his body expelled the bullet then began healing. Other men appeared from behind the house. Roscoe counted twenty in all. He had worse odds in France. He waited until they were all close before he went to work. Roscoe stabbed, cut, and slashed his way through the bodyguards, every blow a killing blow. Thirteen bodies lay sprawled on the ground before the others realized this was no ordinary man they were dealing with. They tried to run, but Roscoe caught them then dragged them back to his blade. He managed to glance toward the house; he saw a car pull from the back then speed up the narrow road. He looked about; five men were still alive, each running in a different direction. If he wanted to get Miss Liza's daughter, he would have to let them go.

He wiped his knife on his pants and tucked it in the back of his pants. Roscoe started with a slow gait then picked up the pace with each step. He ran down the dirt road onto the paved street, increasing his speed. Soon the rear lights of the car came into view. Roscoe ran faster; in a few moments he was side by side with the car, peering into the passenger's window. A young woman sat there; she looked up, saw him and screamed. The driver swerved then looked at him as well. Roscoe lowered his shoulder, ramming it into the car. The driver lost control, the car spinning across the road and into the surrounding marsh. Roscoe hurried to the car. The driver leaned over the steering wheel rubbing his head. The woman looked at him as if he was death. He reached for the door, but the woman locked it. Roscoe gripped the door handle then ripped the door free.

"Don't be afraid," Roscoe said. "Your mama sent me."

The man in the driver's seat pulled out a gun. Roscoe snatched the woman from her seat and turned his back as the man fired. The bullets struck him hard, and he fell forward. He caught himself, hovering over the young woman. He heard the man grunt as he exited the car.

"Get up and turn around," the man ordered.

Roscoe sprang up, knocking the gun from the man's grip. He wrapped his hand around the man's throat then lifted him off his feet.

"Now you listen to me Leonard, and you listen good," Roscoe said. "I'm taking Mary Ann to her mother where she belongs. Y'all could have worked things out, but I guess it's way beyond that now."

"I'm her father!" Leonard said.

"You done took everything from Miss Liza. You ain't going to take her daughter, too. Now I'm going to put you down and you're going to get in that car and keep driving until you get back to where you came from. And you ain't never going tell anybody what happened here. If you do, I'll find out and come for you. And the next time I won't be so nice."

Roscoe set Leonard down on his feet. He glanced at Mary Ann then scrambled to the car, started the engine, then sped into the darkness. When Roscoe turned to the woman she cowered.

"Don't hurt me!" she said.

Roscoe reached into his jacket then took out the letter Miss Liza sent with him.

"This is from your mama," he said.

Mary Ann reached out with a trembling hand then took the letter. She opened it; as she read it her fear gave way to joy. She folded the letter.

"So, you're Roscoe," she said. "Mama told me a lot about you, but I guess not everything."

Roscoe nodded. "You can't tell what you don't know. I'm trusting that you can keep a secret."

"I can," Mary Ann said.

"Good. Now let's get you to New York."

Roscoe picked up the woman.

"Hold on tight," he said.

Mary Ann held his neck tight, and Roscoe sprinted down the road back to Percy's truck. The man was snoring.

"Percy!"

Percy jumped, his eyes wide.

"Where? What?"

He looked at Roscoe and the woman and his eyes got bigger.

"Where the hell you get that white woman from?"

"I'm not white," Mary Ann said.

Roscoe walked over to the passenger's side then put the woman into the truck.

"You'll be alright now," he said.

Mary Ann reached around his neck, pulled him close, then kissed his cheek.

"Thank you, Roscoe," she said.

Roscoe nodded then walked back to the passenger side. He gave Percy ten dollars.

"Percy, this is Miss Mary Ann Pritchard. You take this woman to the train station and stay with her until she boards," Roscoe said.

"Where you going?"

"I got some cleaning up to do."

Percy nodded. "Got it."

Percy sped off down the road. The woman looked back at Roscoe with a warm smile, waving as the pickup truck disappeared into the darkness.

Roscoe returned to Wallace plantation. He found his shovel then dug a deep hole. He piled all the dead men into the hole and covered it the best he could. The sun was breaking in the eastern horizon as he finished. This was a sloppy job, but he didn't have time to make it right. Word would spread soon on what happened at Wallace Plantation and he would need to be long gone by then. He heaved the shovel far into the marsh, and ran into the forest shadows.

* * *

Franklin Stevens took off the blood-stained apron then washed his hands. Working at the slaughterhouse wasn't the best job he'd ever had but it definitely wasn't the worst. He was working, which during these times was a blessing. He trudged to his locker, opened it then took out his coat, hat and scarf. Chicago winters were brutal, and this one was no exception. Despite the cold he walked back to his flat, relishing the quiet time. Sometimes a man just needed to be alone with his thoughts.

His landlord stood in the lobby as he entered the building. He had a sly smile on his face that bothered Franklin.

"Rent due?" he asked.

"No," the landlord replied.

"So why you looking at me like that?"

The landlord grinned. "You'll see."

Franklin shook his head then climbed the stairs to the third floor. He opened his door then stepped inside. He took off his coat and scarf, hanging them on the coat stand near the door.

"Roscoe?"

He stiffened at the sound of an old name from a familiar voice.

He turned around to see Miss Liza sitting at his table.

"Miss Liza," he said. "What are you doing here?"

"It took me a long time and a lot of money to find you," she said.

Roscoe took off his hat. Miss Liza stood then rushed him, wrapping him in a tight hug.

"Thank you so much for sending my baby back to me!"

Roscoe held Miss Liza for a moment then let her go. He walked over to the door then opened it.

"You're welcome. Now I think you best be leaving."

Miss Liza seemed startled.

"Leaving? I just found you! I have so much to tell you, so many questions to ask…"

"I can't answer your questions and there's nothing I need to hear," he said. "I know both of y'all is alright. You know I'm alright. That's got to be enough."

"Roscoe, please."

Roscoe shook his head.

"I'm suspecting Mary Ann told you everything."

Miss Liza's face became serious. "Yes."

"The more you know about me, the less safe you are. There are people out there looking for me and I'm trying my best not to be found. You understand?"

Miss Liza nodded. "I found you."

"Which is why I'm going to leave this place."

Miss Liza gathered her things then walked to the door. She placed her hand on Roscoe's cheek then kissed him.

"You take care of yourself, Roscoe. If you ever get tired of hiding, you have a home with me and Mary Ann."

Roscoe closed his eyes hard to cut off the tears he knew were coming.

"Goodbye, Miss Liza."

Miss Liza's hand lingered on his cheek a moment longer before she left his flat. He closed the door then sat hard at his table. He gave himself a moment, letting a few tears fall before wiping his face. He went to his closet then opened his trunk, gazing at the old uniform and the bolo knife.

"One day," he whispered. "One day."

He took his clothes off the hangers and began to pack.

Undercurrents

Harry loitered on the wharf, staring across Buckra Creek into the empty stinking marsh. An ocean breeze bent the grasses while playing the rusted hoisting cables above him like wind chimes. He'd come full circle, an island boy in the beginning and an island boy in the end. Sadness should have ruled him and would have in Atlanta, where failure stood out like a neon sign against the high-rise monuments to success. But Boot Island was another world, languishing off the Georgia coast like a comforting lover wading in the brackish sea, eager to embrace broken souls like his.

He leaned back on his calloused hands, letting his attention synch with the rhythm of the warning lights flicking on the distant bridge to the mainland. He should have never gone to the city. From the time he stepped off the bus twenty years ago at the Greyhound station on International he was overwhelmed by the city's energetic ambition. His dream of earning a business degree and owning a small business was an anemic desire compared to the wealth and success taunting him. College became a hectic mixture of classrooms and intern boardrooms culminating in a summa cum laude business degree and a starting job most graduates would envy. The next fifteen years were a blur of long days and short nights, hard deals and harder acquisitions with time squeezed in to marry and start a family. Ultimate success was in sight when the recession hit. Harry was cast out like garbage, the downsizing damaging his soul more than his reputation. The rest was his doing, the bankruptcy, the divorce and the drugs. An arrest for possession with intent to distribute one sultry July night at Little Five Points landed him in jail, a harsh slap back to reality. After nine months and an early release he fled the city and returned to the island, not as the success he wanted to be, but the failure that he was.

The wind shifted, the acrid sulfur aroma of the nearby pulpwood plant overwhelming the organic musk of the marsh. Harry crinkled his broad nose and stood, straightening out his white linen pants and tucking in his pale blue polo shirt. At least nature had been kind to him, blessing him with a physique most men his age could barely remember. Among the middle-aged visitors and retirees of the island he was a mid-life black Adonis. His was a profile that brought glances and leers, masking the aura of his disappointment.

He decided to ride to Driftwood Beach. The smell of the paper mill never reached the secluded beach, and he needed the exercise. He climbed onto his rented bike and set off, speeding through the live oaks, grey tendrils of Spanish moss brushing his head. As he pedaled, his thoughts drifted back to his last days in the city.

* * *

"You don't have to do this," his lawyer recommended the day before the bankruptcy proceedings.

"I know, Kelly," he replied. "I just want it to be over with."

Kelly ran his hand across his bald head. "Look, Harry, I've gone over the situation and it's not as bad as it seems. All you need is a few loans to tide you over for a year. I know you have the contacts."

Harry threw up his hands. "I'm tired, Kelly. I don't want to fight anymore. I'll sell you the business and you get the loans. How does that sound?"

Kelly played with his glasses. "Well damn, Harry! I'm not sure I'm capable . . ."

"I thought so," he said. "Come on, let's get this over with. I need to go home."

* * *

The asphalt ended, replaced by the tabby stone road leading to the wooden bridge spanning Jay's Creek. He got off the bike and leaned it against a gnarled scrub pine. He took off his shoes, tied the laces together and hung them on the handlebars. No one would take them, and if they did, he didn't care.

Harry ambled across the bridge, savoring the smooth wood against his feet and the intrusion of the hard-packed sand between his toes. Minutes later he was on the beach, the muted roar of the waves familiar and soothing. Bleached driftwood strewn around him triggered memories from long ago when he scampered like a crab on the same sand as a boy, hunting for perfect shells while avoiding beached jellyfish and sharp seashell fragments. He'd intended to walk only a few miles then spend the rest of the day hunting for a job, but the longer he walked the more reluctant he was to leave.

Harry followed the beach around the northern end of the island to the wind-blown ocean side. Oak trees lined the dune, their canopies yielding permanently to the relentless ocean winds. Farther down he traversed the public beach where the dunes were sheltered by wiregrass and gazebos. Harry remembered the old shacks that used to stand there, homes of the descendants of the slaves that ran to Boot Island for freedom before the Civil War. The people were all gone, driven away by the progress that was supposed to help them, unable to pay the property taxes gentrification demanded.

A mile farther down the beach Harry reached his destination. The house was the only one still on the beach, built in the 1890's by some early industrialist no one re-membered. Harry had spent half his life between its hardwood walls, the only child kept separate from his poorer neighbors, his only companion the vastness undulating before him. The scene seeped through his pores, calming his mind by pulling free memories of simpler times. He remembered endless hours of ocean tag, running back and forth with the waves in childish enthusiasm. Later he would swim, wrapped in the salty splendor of the gray waters. It was too cold to swim now; the warm air of March had yet to penetrate the ocean currents. He thought of going up to the house but decided against it. He had no idea who owned it now, whether it was habitable or a historic site. The beach was close enough. His legs suddenly tired so he sat on the dune, lay back, closed his eyes and dozed off.

Something wet touched his cheek and he jumped awake, his eyes struggling to focus. A smiling face hovered over him, a visage with sparkling sea-green eyes bordered by translucent silver hair. He blinked, and the face became more coherent; a small, almost invisible nose resting perfectly over full, pouting lips. She crouched beside him; her fingers buried in the sand. Her voluptuous body sheathed by a sundress clinging to her curves.

Harry shuffled back. Who the hell was this? A lesser man would see the situation as the beginning of some fantasy encounter. But if life had taught him anything, it was to be wary of dreams come true.

"Who are you?" he managed to ask.

The woman answered him with a frown. She dropped her head, her hair cascading over her shoulders.

"You don't remember me?" she said in a sweet fragile voice.

"I've never seen you before in my life." He pinched himself, hoping for the woman to disappear as he woke from the dream. The pain came but the woman remained, her features as clear as before.

"We spent so much time together," she said. Her voice had become deep and powerful, soothing in its pitch. She rose, exposing her perfection as she walked away with unnatural grace. Harry watched her, his breath falling into the rhythm of each step, each sway of her wide hips. She was almost to the water when she spun about and ran towards him. Harry's heart jumped, and he ran to her. Before he could reach her, she turned then ran away. He slowed to a trot, a grin coming to his face. She stopped and ran back again, and Harry was startled. She was playing ocean tag with him.

"We used to do this for hours," she said. Harry was shaken by a wave of anger. Who was this woman who knew his private moments? She was too young to have been alive then. Someone must have told her these things, but whom?

She turned to face him. "Remember when you gave me this?"

She held out her left hand. On her finger was the ring. Vertigo seized him and his arms flailed for support. One hand landed on her shoulder, and she grabbed him with amazing strength. Harry's mind fled twenty-two years away, painfully reliving the betrayal that pushed him to the beach that autumn night, holding that same ring like some disgusting piece of trash. He threw it as far as he could into the pulsing surf, deciding at that moment he would leave Boot Island and make something of himself. Success was the best revenge, he thought.

The strange woman wore the ring, this person with the boundless eyes, who emitted a sense of rhythm while standing still, who held onto his memories like discarded jewels. An answer came to him that he quickly dismissed as absurd, the result of a wounded mind. He pulled away from her.

"I don't know how you found out all those things about me and I don't want to know," he said. "Please go."

"I can't," she replied. "I'm here for you. I always have been. I always will be."

Harry didn't hear her last words. He was running, his legs laboring against the soft sand, tufts of dirt kicked up by his rapid feet. He fled across the beach and bridge, abandoning his bike and shoes and ignoring the fire in his chest as his lungs struggled for respite. He broke his stride when he reached his bungalow. Harry collapsed against the door, overcome by fatigue and the fear that he was going mad.

He fumbled for his keys, unlocked the door, and stumbled in. He ransacked the room until he found his cognac. He guzzled it out the bottle, rivulets of the liquor running down his cheeks and onto his shirt, the smooth heat inside bringing him back to his senses. He dropped the bottle and collapsed on his bed, searching for and finally finding enough calm inside himself to sleep.

Morning brought throbbing ache and stabbing sunlight. Harry rose from the bed too quickly and fell, his head banging against the old particle wood dresser. He lay there a moment in paralyzing pain, shit-faced like a damn college freshman. Pulling himself up to a squat, he looked around the room to get his bearings. The thought of breakfast made him nauseous. He had to do something to get rid of the headache. A swim was what he needed, a nice long swim.

Harry made his way to the southern tip of the island, gathering his bike and shoes along the way. He convinced himself that the incident on the beach the day before had been pure illusion. He laughed out loud, the bike jiggling its way to the beach across jagged pavement.

This was a quiet beach, hidden from tourists by a palisade of water oaks guarding high dunes covered with sea grass. Harry worked his way through the palmettos and prickly pears, tossing the bike aside as he reached the short stretch of marsh separating the trees from the dunes. Pulling himself through the tangle of grass and mud, he climbed the dunes then stumbled down the steep sides to the deserted beach. The ocean played its ancient tune against the hard-packed sand. Harry swayed, entwined by the rhythm of the waves. Standing near the beach, the endless fathoms before him, the pull was irresistible. He shed his clothes then staggered into the water. The chill sobered him, the waves lapping against his calves, his thighs, up to his waist. He lunged into the surf and swam. It was the only place he ever felt alone. His only concern was the rhythm, the stroke of his arms, the kick of his legs and the crest and trough of the waves. Success did not matter here; wealth was no concern; only a man and the sea and the timeless cadence.

His chest tingled, the signal that his limit was near, but Harry kept swimming. He wanted to keep going, to be swallowed into infinity, his problems and failures lost in the waters before and below him. He swam on, each stroke long and laborious, the increasing pain like a blow with each stroke. But he would not stop. He heard the call of the ocean and understood its meaning. With his last effort he turned onto his back, flinging his arms out and opening his mouth.

The sea consumed him, rushing around his limbs and torso, filling his mouth and nose. But he did not choke, nor did he sink. The waves cradled and rocked him, the brackish fluid in his lungs like a lover's breath. The movement was sensual, and Harry was aroused. He should have been drowning but he wasn't. Was this what death felt like? Was this the final ecstasy before the loss of his soul, the vanguard of the light? It didn't matter. Embraced in the buoyant bosom of the sea he felt content. Money could not buy this; power could not equal it. It existed in the waves and the tides and the foam. It ran through his lungs and stroked his skin. It was his before he left, it was his again. Harry closed his eyes and slipped into intimate darkness.

He stirred, sand grinding against his back. A seagull's lament rose from a distance, its cry expressing its disappointment. He cracked open his eyes and sunlight seeped in, driving away the clouded dregs of his last thoughts. Why wasn't he dead?

The answer hovered above him. The woman loomed like a cloud, her sea-green eyes bright with emotion.

"You saved me," he said.

"Yes."

Harry sat up, shaking his head. "I didn't see you. How did you know?"

"You were inside me," she said. "I would never let you die there."

Harry's head spun as he tried to understand her answer. She knelt before him, placing her delicate hand on his grizzled cheek.

"We are bonded, you and me. We are part of each other. The reason is irrelevant. The truth is all that matters."

She leaned forward and kissed him hard. He was swept away by the same rush he felt when he was drowning and now he understood its source. The kiss ended too quickly; she withdrew from him and backed away to the edge of the surf.

"Do not leave me again," she said. "All you need is here." She walked into the waves, merging with the grayish water until she disappeared. Harry waited to see the kick of her legs, perhaps an ankle of her swimming away, but there was only water.

Harry always loved the sea, but never did he imagine she loved him, too. He felt a calmness missing inside him for so long, an emotion he had neglected and ignored when he left for the city to seek something he had right before him all along. The sun appeared from the watery horizon as more gulls heralded its arrival. Harry stood. He walked into the waves, the dampness of his lover caressing his calves.

"I will never leave you again," he whispered. "I promise." He kissed his hand and placed it in the waves, the water swirling around his palm warm and tender. He turned and walked away, leaving his footprints in the sand. She followed him, filling his imprints with herself, and then swept back into the constant, contented waves.

Kaleidoscope

Late Christmas morning. Kerry's breath frosted his bedroom window. He waited anxiously for Uncle John's arrival. Uncle John was his favorite because he always brought the best gifts. Daddy didn't like Uncle John; he would say that Uncle John tried to show up everyone else with his presents. He said if Uncle John had kids of his own, he wouldn't be able to afford those gifts. Kerry didn't care; he just wanted his presents. He wished Uncle John never got married.

He sat up straight when he spotted the familiar BMW 745 cruising up the long hill to his house. He jumped off the bed, his feet slamming against the floor as he tore out of his room.

"Uncle John is coming! Uncle John is coming!"

Kerry ran by his sister's room on the way to the stairs. Michelle stuck her head out the door, her rollers tumbling to the floor, her cell phone pressed against her head.

"Girl, I got to go! My Uncle John is coming." She pulled her head back into her room to dress.

Jerome was downstairs. He sat at the table with Daddy, playing with his new laptop. Mama stood before the oven, putting the finishing touches on the slow-cooking Christmas ham. Jerome was graduating and heading off to college soon, so Mama and Daddy bought him a laptop to help him with his work. Kerry didn't like the laptop; Jerome wouldn't let him play any games on it. Kerry ran through the family room and down the foyer to the front door.

"Get away from that door, boy!" Mama exclaimed.

Kerry's hands dropped to his side like a little soldier. "It's Uncle John, Mama. He's coming up the street!"

Mama wiped her hands on her apron and strolled towards the door. "How do you know?"

"I saw him out the window."

"What did I tell you about looking out that window? You're always leaving my blinds up. Move on out the way now."

Mama gently pushed Kerry aside and looked through the peep hole.

"It's John," she said, "and he's got someone with him."

Daddy huffed. "I hope it's not one of his freeloader friends."

Mommy looked back with a sly smile on her face. "It's a woman, a very pretty woman."

Daddy feigned shock. "You're lying!"

The doorbell rang. Mama opened the door with a wide grin.

"Merry Christmas, J!"

Uncle John stepped into the house, lifting Mama off her feet. He was a tall man with brown copper skin and a round joyful face.

"Merry Christmas, big sister!" he announced, his alto voice filling the foyer. He carried Mama back into the foyer and placed her down. A woman entered, an ebony skinned woman draped in a kente colored coat. Her hair was cut close like Uncle John's and her smile was sincere like an old friend.

"Barbara, this is Zarina."

Barbara hugged Zarina. "Welcome to our home, Zarina. You're beautiful."

Zarina lowered her eyes. "You are too kind, Barbara. Thank you for having me. I told John to ask if it was okay that I come, but he insisted. I apologize if my presence is an inconvenience."

Barbara waved her hand. "Not at all, girl. There's plenty for everybody. Besides, you don't look like you eat as much as his other friends."

As the ladies shared a laugh Uncle John noticed Kerry. His eyes widened and he grabbed the boy, lifting him to the ceiling.

"Barbara, what you been feeding this boy? Miracle Gro?" He shook and tickled Kerry at the same time. "What's up, big boy?"

"Stop, Uncle John!" Kerry squealed.

Daddy walked up to them. "How you doing, John?" He stepped past Kerry and Tee to greet Zarina.

"Welcome, Zarina. Y'all come away from this door. It's too cold."

They went to the family room, Uncle John carrying Kerry under his thick arm.

"Where's my present?" Kerry demanded.

"So that's what's going on," Uncle John said. "I thought you were happy to see me. You're just down here for the loot."

"You spoiled him," Daddy said.

Michelle made her entrance, overdressed as always.

"Hi, Uncle John," she said with a shy wave of her hand.

"Girl, get over here and give me hug!"

Michelle shed her teenage pretense and skittered across the floor to hug her uncle.

"Now that's more like it!"

Jerome sauntered up and extended his hand.

"What's up, young man?" His voice was suddenly serious.

"Uncle." They shook and hugged. Kerry looked at them envious. He wished he was old enough to shake and hug Uncle John like that.

"So, you're a college man now?"

Jerome smirked. "Not yet."

"Where you going?"

Jerome stuck his chest out. "Morehouse."

Mama sucked her teeth. "Not unless he gets a scholarship."

"He'll get one," Uncle John replied. "Money ain't a thing." Uncle John reached into his coat pocket and extracted an envelope.

"Merry Christmas, young man."

Kerry ran to his uncle. The presents were here!

Jerome opened the envelope and his eyes bugged. "Thank you, unc! Thank you!"

"That's for college now," Uncle John said. "Don't spend it on gaming."

Mama pushed Kerry aside and took the envelope from Jerome. She looked at the check and her eyes went just as wide.

"Oh my God! J, where did you get this kind of money? We can't accept this!"

Daddy ran over to see for himself. "Oh yes, we can! Let me see." He looked at the check and sat down. "Ten thousand dollars!" he exclaimed. "Now that's what I'm talking about!"

"I got something for you, too," Uncle John said to Michelle. He reached into another pocket and took out an iPhone. Michelle squealed.

"Don't panic, sis. I got the bill."

Uncle John squatted before Kerry. "Your turn little man." Uncle John reached inside his coat. A video pad made its way ceremoniously to Kerry's hand. Kerry hugged Uncle John tight.

"Thank you, Uncle John!"

"You earned it. Your Mama said you're a straight A student. Good work deserves good reward."

Everyone settled into the family room while Mama and Michelle went to the kitchen to finish dinner. Kerry sat down and went to work, immersing himself in his favorite game on the pad. He looked up from time to time when everyone else got loud to see what was happening. Every time his eyes met Zarina's, an admiring smile was on her face. Kerry smiled back and resumed his game.

Kerry was upset when he had to put away his pad for dinner hours later. His anger was brief; the food was excellent. Mama went all out as always, with turkey, ham, dressing, macaroni and cheese casserole, collard greens, sweet potato soufflé, rice, gravy, cranberry sauce and cornbread. It was enough for twice as many people. Jerome, Michelle and Kerry sat together at the kitchen table, listening to Daddy tell his funny stories at the grown-up table. Kerry escaped from the kitchen as soon as he finished his plate, running upstairs to his room to immerse himself in the complexities of Sonic the Hedgehog.

A light tapping on his door broke his attention.

"Yes?" Kerry yelled out.

"Can I come in?" an unfamiliar voice asked.

Kerry rolled off his bed reluctantly and opened the door. Zarina stood before him, a sweet smile on her face.

"You ran away before I could give you your gift."

Kerry's eyes brightened. Zarina handed him a leather tube etched with images of elephants and lions. Kerry was confused.

"Open it," Zarina said.

Kerry opened the tube and extracted a wooden object that looked like a telescope.

Kerry studied it.

"It's a kaleidoscope." Zarina took the object from him. "See, you put this end to your eye and turn this end. Try it."

Kerry placed the kaleidoscope to his eye. Inside was a colorful pattern of colored crystals. When he turned the large end, the pattern changed. He smiled. "It's like the snowflakes in my class," he said.

Zarina smiled. "Very good, Kerry. John told me you were smart."

Kerry kept turning the kaleidoscope. It wasn't very fun, not like his game, but Mama told him to always be polite.

"Are you going to marry my uncle?"

Zarina laughed. "Your uncle is a nice man, but I don't think we'll marry. I'm too old for him."

Kerry lowered the kaleidoscope and studied Miss Zarina.

"You don't look THAT old," he said.

"You'd be surprised," Zarina replied.

She folded her arms. "Now it's time for a secret. Tonight, when everyone is asleep, I want you to take the kaleidoscope and go to your window. Before you look inside, I want you to close your eyes and say, 'Wherever I see, I can be.'"

"Mama doesn't like me looking out the window," he warned.

"She won't know if you close the blinds," Zarina answered. "Now what are you going to say?"

"Wherever I see, I can be," Kerry recited.

Zarina smiled like a proud teacher. "Good. I'll leave you to your games. Goodbye, Kerry. I hope to see you again one day."

Kerry tossed the kaleidoscope on the bed and continued his game. He stopped for a moment to go downstairs for pound cake and vanilla ice cream, then it was back to his room. He barely noticed Uncle John stick his head in to say goodbye. After being forced to bathe, Kerry played until his eyes became too heavy to stay open. He fell asleep, the pad still in his grip.

He awoke suddenly, the words Zarina taught him buzzing in his head. Kerry went to the window and lifted the blinds, the kaleidoscope in his sleepy fingers. He lifted it to his eye, the colorful patterns boring to him.

"Wherever I see, I can be," he whispered.

He turned the large end and the crystals disappeared, replaced by a montage of space and stars.

"Wow!" He turned it again and a solar system appeared, five planets circling a yellow star similar to the sun. Two of the planets occupied the same orbit, one directly opposite the other. Both planets had the same color of Earth. He twisted the big end and a planet appeared in closeup, the surface covered with trees and grasses, mountains towering into the sky, flying things and walking things and crawling things in abundance. But these were not the trees and animals that he knew. He turned it again and this time he saw people that reminded him of Zarina, working and playing in cities that were again the same, but different. He kept turning the kaleidoscope, marveling at the amazing images. *This is better than the pad*, he thought.

Kerry twisted. The planets were gone. He was looking at space again, at stars cast on the infinite black void. A luminous blue line appeared, connecting stars like dots while numbers flashed before his eyes.

"Cool!" he said. He gazed into the toy so long that the sun finally peeked over the hills.

"Uh oh!" Kerry closed the blinds and jumped into bed. He looked into the kaleidoscope. The crystals had returned.

"Only at night," he whispered. He placed the toy on his dresser and fell asleep.

* * *

Reporters from around the world flooded Cape Canaveral, each hoping to get a close view of the podium. The usual dignitaries occupied the choice seats and each one was claimed. No one wanted to miss what promised to be the most historic day for mankind.

The press secretary took the podium, brushing her hair back from her beaming face. Despite her years of announcing scientific breakthroughs, she exuded an unexpected joyfulness that was reflected by the anxious throng.

"Ladies and gentlemen, I don't have much to say. You all have followed this project since its start eight years ago. None of us imagined it would culminate so quickly, but all of us are ecstatic about the outcome and the man who made it happen. I won't make you wait any longer. Let me introduce the man of the hour, the adventurer that will take us into a new age of space travel, Colonel Kerry Washington!"

The conference room exploded in applause. Colonel Washington took the stage in his flight suit, waving at the crowd. He hugged the press secretary and took the podium.

"I'd like to say a few words before I take any questions. This dream began for me when I was a little boy. I stand here today realizing a dream come true. When our brilliant team of scientists transformed the theory of slip dimensional travel to reality, the stars opened up to us. The journey I embark on this day will prove once and for all we are not alone."

Stacy Owens, Technology correspondent for the New York Times, sprang to her feet.

"How can you be so sure, Colonel? What makes you believe you can find intelligent life?"

Kerry just smiled, refusing to answer the reporter's question. Later that day as he strapped himself into the *Traveler*, he thought about that Christmas day when he received a special gift from a special person.

"How do I know what I'll find?" he said to himself. "Because I know exactly where I'm going."

He checked his instruments one last time then gave Mission Control the signal to begin launch sequence. In an afterthought he reached into his pocket and pulled out a worn kaleidoscope, securing it atop the panel.

"Wherever I see, I can be," he whispered.

Grandpa's Hands

Michael felt heat radiating from his wood-paneled bedroom wall and sprang from his bed. The smell of bacon wafted into his room as he hurried into the jeans and sweatshirt he set out the night before, wrestled on his tennis shoes, and trotted through the narrow hallway into the kitchen. Mama stood before the stove, one hand holding the black iron skillet in place while the other scrambled a pair of eggs in a hot pool of bacon grease.

"What you doing up so early, boy?" she asked without looking.

Michael sat at the dinette, folding his eager hands under his chin. "You going to Grandma's?" he asked.

Mama scraped the scrambled eggs onto a plate. "I go out there every Saturday morning. You know that."

Michael played with the napkin holder, rocking his head from side to side. "Can I go?"

Mama was reaching for the grits but stopped, placing her small hands on her broad hips. "Now why in the world do you want to go with me?"

"Because I want to go hunting."

Mama rolled her eyes. "You and that gun. I told your daddy not to buy you that thing unless he was ready to go hunting with you. His tired behind ain't been out with you yet."

She scooped a spoonful of grits on the plate to join the eggs and bacon. "You know you can't go by yourself, and your daddy ain't waking up any time soon."

Michael smothered his grits with pepper. "Uncle Willy will take me."

"How you know he's going hunting today? This close to harvest time, he's probably got chores."

Michael piled his eggs on top of his grits with the

pepper and crumbled the bacon in his hands. "I called him last night, and he said he was going."

Mama turned around and looked at him, her eyes wide. "You did what?" She shook her head. "Lord, lord, what I'm gonna do with you?"

She began to make her own plate then stopped. "What about that book report you supposed to be working on? You finished it yet?"

"No, ma'am."

"No? Then how you expect to go with me if you got homework to do?"

"I'll finish it as soon as I get home, Mama, I promise."

Mama turned to look at Michael.

"What you writing about?"

Michael spread apple jelly on his toast.

"I'm supposed to write about my hero. I'm thinking about Frederick Douglass."

Michael finished his plate before Mama sat down.

"I guess you can go," she said. "But we ain't leaving until I'm ready to leave, you hear me?"

"Yes, ma'am!"

"And I want to see that book report after church tomorrow."

"Yes, ma'am"

Michael jumped from the table and ran to Mama and Daddy's room to get the .22 rifle. He hoarded his lawn-cutting money all summer to buy it as a birthday present to himself. It was a Springfield/Savage .22 semiautomatic long rifle, the perfect gun for squirrel and rabbit hunting, or so the salesclerk at Sears said. Michael eased the door open and crept to the closet beside the bed. Daddy was stretched out on top of the covers in his boxer shorts and t-shirt, snoring through his thick moustache. The closet door creaked when Michael slid it aside, and Daddy's hand came up to scratch his side-burns. Michael froze until he stopped scratching then slid the door wide open. The gun was hidden behind Mama's Sunday dresses. He took it out then went to Daddy's loose-change drawer where he kept the bullets. There was a brand-new pack of one hundred shells that felt like money in the boy's hands.

Michael strode into the kitchen, carrying the rifle the way Daddy taught him. Mama looked up from her cup of coffee and grinned despite herself.

"You look like your Uncle Bo when he was your age," she said. She got up from the table and headed for the bedroom. "Guess I better get ready. The day ain't getting no longer."

Michael washed his plate then went to the den. He laid his gun down on the floor and turned on the TV to watch cartoons. He'd almost forgotten about going with Mama when she came into the den.

"Cut that mess off and let's go," she said.

Michael scrambled to his feet, turned off the TV, and grabbed the gun and bullets.

"Now remember what I said. We don't leave 'til I'm ready."

"Yes, ma'am."

"And if your Uncle Willy can't take you hunting, you don't go."

"Yes, ma'am."

"All right then, let's go."

Michael trailed Mama out the door into the carport and into the '67 sky blue Malibu. In moments, they were zooming through the neighborhood down the steep hills between the little water oaks the city planted to beautify the landscape. Mama worked her way through the side streets and shortcuts with the serious-ness of a NASCAR driver, reaching Macon Road, the two-lane highway that ran right to Grandma's farm. The sky was a crisp autumn blue, empty of the gray haze that sagged low during the summer. The morning sun spread its light across the pine-infested hills. It felt like hunting season, and Michael was excited. He watched the familiar landmarks flash by from his backseat window until he saw the solitary shack that signaled the farm wasn't far away. Mama finally slowed down as the roadside mailboxes came into view. She steered off the paved highway and onto the dirt road. She was creeping as they approached the railroad crossing. Only the section crossing the road was visible, the rest blocked by a tangle of scrub pines and honeysuckle vines.

Mama turned left after crossing the tracks. She drove through a gauntlet of blackberry vines that made Michael's mouth water as he remembered blackberry pie and ice cream. They turned right at the hog pens. The house appeared, flanked by the corn and peas fields. Mama drove down the road to the rear of the house, parking between the house and the shed. Michael jumped out of the car before Mama came to a complete stop, his impatient eyes searching for Uncle Willy. His euphoria was checked by a jerk of his arm that almost lifted him off his feet.

"Boy, don't you ever jump out that car like that again!" Mama's face was get-me-a-switch angry.

"Don't go hitting that boy," a much older female voice growled. Grandma stood at the screen door of the back patio. Michael blessed her for saving him from what was surely going to be a whupping or at least a pinch on the arm. She eased down the concrete stairs, wiping her hands on her apron.

"Did you see what he did?" Mama said.

"He ain't hurt. You'll know better the next time, won't you, Michael?"

87

"Yes ma'am."

Michael followed Mama and Grandma up the stairs. Since he'd made Mama mad, he sat beside the women on an old folding chair, took his share of butterbeans from the bushel, and began shelling. He kept his eyes low, and peeled while they talked, waiting for the right moment to ask the question that was burning to get out of his throat.

Mama stopped talking as she grabbed another handful of beans. Michael cleared his throat and looked up at Grandma.

"Grandma, is Uncle Willy here?"

"Shoot boy, Willy went hunting right about sunup. He won't be back until dark."

Michael slumped over like he'd been hit by a brick. He looked at Mama with pleading eyes.

"I told you no hunting by yourself with that gun," she reminded him.

"I'll take him."

Grandpa shuffled in from the kitchen, his hands deep in his overall pockets. He smiled at Michael, flashing his gold tooth, and Michael was filled with dread.

"You feel like hunting, Daddy?" Mama asked. "You're supposed to be resting."

"I don't want to go hunting no more," Michael whispered.

"I feel fine," Grandpa replied, pulling his right hand out of his pocket. Michael watched the gnarled, scarred appendage rise to the old man's bald head. It was hideous, like something from the freak show at the fair. When he was small, he was always careful to avoid touching or being touched by that hand and its mirror twin. He thought when he was older, he'd get over the fear, but it was still clinging to him as real as ever.

"I don't want to go hunting no more," he said

louder.

"Is it all right?" Mama asked Grandma.

Grandma concentrated on the peas. "The doctor said he needed to get some exercise."

"I don't want to go no more!" Michael shouted.

"Boy, can't you see grown folks talking?" Mama nailed him still with her stare then returned to her conversation.

"Well, Papa, I guess it's okay, but you keep a close eye on him. He can get wild sometimes."

"What you mean 'you guess it's okay?'" Grandpa said. "I'll take this boy anywhere I want to. Come on, Michael. Let's go hunting."

Michael watched the back of Grandpa's head as he bounced down the stairs. He looked at Mama in desperation.

"What you waiting on? Go on now."

Michael turned and followed Grandpa down the stairs. He could do this; he was twelve going on thirteen with two hairs on his chest and the start of a moustache on his upper lip. His confidence had almost returned until he caught a glimpse of those hands pull out a pouch of Red Man chewing tobacco. He jumped past Grandpa and trotted to the car to get his .22.

"What you gonna kill with that? Time?"

Michael ignored the comment, holding the gun towards the ground like his Daddy taught him and making sure the safety was on.

"Squirrels and rabbits, sir," he said.

Grandpa laughed like a wet growl. "Can't kill no squirrels with that thing. Ain't gonna do nothing but make them mad. I should've brought my shotgun."

Grandpa started walking, and Michael followed, afraid to say where he wanted to hunt. They followed a trail branching off the dirt road that cut between the barn and the old mule stables.

"No, can't kill nothing with that thing," Grandpa continued. "Can't kill it right, I mean. You shoot a squirrel with that and it'll be running around mad, hurting, and hiding. A shotgun will put it down just like that."

Grandpa stopped walking, and Michael almost ran into him.

"See this?" he asked, pointing at a dent between his right thumb and finger. "Shot a squirrel one time and thought it was dead. I guess I should have asked it before I went to picking it up. Damn thing took hold to me right here like a beaver trap. Took a half an hour to get it loose, and it was dead half that time."

Michael looked at the spot and grimaced, imagining how painful that must have felt. Suddenly the scar and the hand were gone, sinking deep into Grandpa's pocket.

They walked to the second hog pen where the trail ended, the air heavy with the stink of swamp mud and hog droppings. Before them was the turnip green field, the fall planting full and ready for harvest. Grandpa walked into the field and over to the barbed wire fence separating the field from the woods. Michael hadn't planned on going into those trees. It was a tangle of pines, oaks, and muscadine vines that seemed perpetually dark as it repulsed the sun's attempts to penetrate its core. Blind obedience only went so far.

"Grandpa, are we going in there?"

"You want to shoot squirrels, don't you?"

Michael reluctantly nodded his head.

"Well, this is the best spot for them; at least it was a while back. Come over here and hold this wire down for me."

Michael sat the gun down on the opposite side of the fence then grabbed the wire carefully, pushing down with his weight. Grandpa stepped over, his hand gripping Michael's shoulder for support. Michael closed his eyes, keeping his head away from the hand.

"Got to be careful," Grandpa said as he grunted his way over the fence. Once he and Michael were settled, he showed his left hand.

"When I was about your Uncle Willy's age, I worked for a white man named Mr. Elias Burnside in his sawmill. It was hard work back then because a colored man did whatever the boss man said do, even if it wasn't your job. Well, one day I was putting up a fence like this one on Mr. Burnside's farm, and before I knew it, I was up to my ankles in fire ants. Boy, I got to jumping around and screaming and tore my hand up on that barbed wire. Took me a long time to get this hand back straight."

Michael climbed over the fence. The woods towered before them in black silence, its stillness a final warning to all intruders. Michael's eyes went to Grandpa, waiting for him to lead the way. Instead, Grandpa reached into his pocket, pulled out his Red Man chewing tobacco, and leaned against the fence post.

"We stay here and wait," Grandpa said. "They'll come to us."

Michael never dreamed a more terrible fate. In front of him were the scariest woods on the farm, and beside him was Grandpa. He sat with the rifle across his lap as he watched Grandpa massage his hands. They must hurt all the time, he thought. Maybe he was used to it; the pain was there but had become a part of Grandpa's life, like the receding gray hair on his head.

"Why you rubbing your hands, Grandpa?" he asked.

"They get to itching sometimes."

"You got arthritis?"

Grandpa tilted his head up and stared at Michael.

91

"What? Shoot boy, ain't nothing wrong with me but old age. These hands are fine."

He moved close to Michael and turned his right hand up, pointing at thick yellow circles on his palms below each finger.

"This comes from hard work, boy. I got these trophies swinging an axe longer than you been alive."

He turned his hand over and placed his finger on a faint line near his pinky finger.

"This line here? I got this when your mama was born. We didn't have no hospital for colored folks back then, so the midwife comes over from Midland to help deliver her. Your grandma was going through an awful time, so I slipped in the room and told her to bite on my hand till she felt better. Lord Almighty, that woman can bite!"

Grandpa chuckled. Michael stared at Grandpa's hands, trying to make up a story about every indentation, line, scar, and curve. They began a game of show-and-tell, Michael asking and Grandpa telling as the sun passed over them between cotton clouds.

"Where did those come from?" Michael pointed to the twin scars ringing Grandpa's wrists. The glow that had been building in the old man's face fled; he straightened and walked away along the fence.

"Grandpa, wait!" Michael jumped to his feet and grabbed his rifle, running until he caught up. Grandpa hummed, his eyes focused somewhere up ahead. Michael grabbed his arm.

"Come on, Grandpa. Let's go back to the house."

Grandpa jerked his arm away. "You want to know how I got them scars, don't you?"

Michael dropped his head. "Yes, sir."

"Come on with me then," Grandpa said. They walked in silence past the peas to the watermelons.

Grandpa picked a small melon, walked over to a wide tree stump, and eased himself down. He pulled out his pocketknife and began slicing. Michael sat beside him, and Grandpa handed him a glistening red wedge.

"Remember when I told you I worked at Mr. Burnside's mill? Well, I was looking to buy me some land for a farm, and old Burnside heard about it. One day he calls me into his office and offers me this land you're sitting on for five hundred dollars. At first, I thought he was playing with me, but old Burnside had a habit of doing things for people he liked, white or colored. So, I jumped for the deal like a frog to water, giving him a hundred straight out and working out a deal for the other four."

Michael listened as he munched on his melon slice. He imagined Grandpa as a young man, tall and strong like Uncle Willy, pulling logs and plowing fields while fussing at Mama for doing something she wasn't supposed to do. The distance between them melted away; the old man with the crippled hands became a real person, father of Mama and Uncle Willy, husband and provider for Grandma.

"Well," Grandpa continued, "I took to clearing that land every evening after work, sometimes with my brothers, but most the time by myself. One evening, I was alone chopping wood when I see a truck rolling up. By the time I figured out what's going on, it was too late to run. Three white men got out of that truck, and the biggest one had a shotgun."

"'What the hell you doing on this land, boy?' he says. 'This here's my land,' I says."

"'You lying,' the little one says. 'We sold this land to Tom Burnside, so unless you're out here waiting on him, you best be getting on, nigger.'"

"Now I was so mad I couldn't think straight. 'Mr.

Burnside sold me this land,' I yelled. 'I paid for it fair and square.'"

"The big man turned red as fire."

"'That son-of-a-bitch!' he says. He turned to the short one and says, 'I told you not to sell it to that old fool! Everybody knows Tom is crazy.'"

"The short man got this evil grin on his face. 'Ain't no problem,' he said. 'This boy's gonna give our land back to us, ain't you, boy?'"

Grandpa bit into his melon, taking his time to chew. "Now if I hadn't spent so much time clearing and chopping, I would have gave it back. But my sweat was in the ground. It belonged to me."

"'This is my land, and I'm keeping it,' I says."

"The big man starts smirking like the devil's son. 'You'll give it back sooner or later,' he said. I tried to run, but they wrestled me down and knocked me out. When I woke up, I was hanging by my wrists from a big old oak tree. The big man had a long piece of rope wrapped around his hands, and as soon as he saw I was awake, he started tearing into me. I wanted to holler so loud the angels would come down to get me, but when I opened my mouth *Amazing Grace* came out. I sang that song louder than I ever had in church, and I meant it more, too. I tell you, boy, the Lord must have heard your grandpa because by the time I stopped singing that song, them white men was gone. They left me hanging there, swinging back and forth like a broke branch until about dark. That's when my brother showed up looking for me and cut me down."

Michael's hands twisted the stock of his rifle, the veins showing in his forearms. "What did you do to those white men, Grandpa?"

Grandpa looked at Michael with a melancholy smile. "Nothing. Couldn't do a thing. See, back then, the law kept a colored man from being strong on the outside, so you had to be strong in here." He patted Michael's chest with his hand, and Michael didn't mind.

"No, I didn't do nothing to them, but I cut that damn oak tree down!" Grandpa looked at his wrists, turning his hands back and forth. "That's how I got these here scars, and that's how this fine sitting stump came to be."

Grandpa struggled to his feet. "Come on, boy. It's about time we be getting back. Them squirrels looking at us and laughing."

"Okay, Grandpa," Michael said. He grasped Grandpa's hand and pulled himself up. They stood for a moment, his young smooth hand in Grandpa's leathery scarred grip, then they let go and headed for the house.

Mama was putting a bunch of collards into the car trunk when Michael and Grandpa walked up.

"So where are all the squirrels?" she asked.

"In the woods," Grandpa replied. "That's alright though. We'll get them next time, right, Michael?"

"Yes, sir, we sure will."

"Get in the car, baby," Mama said.

Michael emptied the .22 and placed it in the trunk beside the collards. He sat on the passenger side as Mama hugged Grandpa's neck.

"Bye, Daddy. I love you."

Grandpa grunted and walked towards the house. Mama climbed in the car with a smile.

"That man is something else," she said.

Mama started the car, and they drove away down the road. Michael turned to see Grandpa waving goodbye. He smiled and waved back until Grandpa disappeared with distance and dust.

"Mama, I ain't writing about Frederick Douglass,"

Michael said.

"Who you writing about?" she asked.

"I'm writing about Grandpa."

Mama turned to look at Michael, her eyes glistening as she smiled at him.

"Lord have mercy," she said. "Lord have mercy."

The Big One

"Come on boy. We goin' fishing."

Uncle Frank patted Cecil's head as he walked across the front porch to the screen door. Cecil jumped to his feet, following his uncle as he swayed into the kitchen. Mama was hovering over the stove, scooping the last bit of grits out the old pot while daddy sat at the dinette reading the Columbus Ledger. Mama turned and looked at her wayward brother; daddy folded the newspaper just enough to see him.

"What you doing here so early, Franky?" mama asked.

"Goin' fishing," Franky replied. "Taking Cecil with me if you let me."

Uncle Franky pulled out a chair from the dinette and almost fell trying to sit. Daddy folded his paper and set it down.

"You been drinking?" he asked.

"Naw man!" Uncle Frank replied. "Just a little unstable this morning. You know how it is when you get my age. I think it's a sinus condition."

"Since when did they start calling Jack Daniel's a sinus condition?" Daddy said.

Mama sat a cup of coffee in front of Uncle Frank.

"Just in case your sinuses get worse," she said.

"I appreciate you, Jennette," said Uncle Frank.

Cecil laughed as he peered through the screen door. Uncle Frank was always doing something funny. Mama didn't think he was funny, but daddy would sit around with him, laughing until he cried.

Uncle Frank looked at him and winked.

"You got any bait?" he asked.

"No, sir," Cecil said.

"That's alright," Uncle Frank said. "We'll get some on the way."

"Where y'all going? Mount Vernon? Eagle Phoenix Mill?"

"Nope. We're going to the Church Lake."

Daddy sucked his teeth. "Ain't no fish in that lake."

"What you mean is that you can't catch no fish in that lake," Uncle Frank replied. "You just ain't holding your mouth right."

"How long y'all gonna be?" Mama asked.

"Now you know I don't come back until I caught something."

"They'll be back next week," Daddy said.

"Go to hell, Sam," Uncle Frank said. Cecil covered his mouth as he laughed.

"Don't be cussing around the boy," mama said.

"'Scuse me young man," Uncle Frank said with a wink. Cecil winked back. He'd heard Uncle Frank say a lot worse when he lost a fish.

Uncle Frank finished his coffee then stood.

"We better get going," he said. "Them fish getting bored waiting for us.

Mama came to Cecil, firmly clasping his cheeks between her warm hands. Cecil tried to pull away, but mama's grip was mama's grip. She kissed his forehead.

"You have fun, baby," she said.

"Yes, ma'am," he replied as he wiped his forehead.

"You know that boy is too old for you to be kissing him," Uncle Frank said.

"You mind your business, Franky," Mama said. "I'll be smacking that forehead as long as I'm alive."

Uncle Frank shook his head. "Come on, boy. Let's catch some fish."

Cecil followed Uncle Frank to his '55 Chevy pickup. The boy opened the door. A pile of potato chip bags was

98

on the passenger side. Cecil swept them onto the floor.
He climbed in and slammed the door just like Uncle
Frank taught him. After three tries the truck rumbled to
life and they were on their way.

Uncle Frank drove to Jackson's Bait Shop, an old
building near Mr. Jackson's main business, Jay's Junk
Yard. Tiffany Jackson, Mr. Jackson's sister, was behind
the counter sipping an RC Cola while humming with an
Al Green song playing on the radio. Uncle Frank took
off his Braves cap and patted his hair before throwing
open the screen door.

"Hey, Tiffy!"

Miss Tiffany turned, and a wide smile came to her
face.

"Well, well, well. Look what the cat dragged in.
Where you been, man?"

Miss Tiffany came from behind the counter, gave Uncle Frank a hug, then straight-up kissed him.

"Ugh," Cecil said as he covered his eyes.

Uncle Frank and Tiffany laughed.

"Hey, little man!" Tiffany said. "You gonna out fish
your uncle again?"

"Yes, ma'am," Cecil said.

"Why you asking him that?" Uncle Frank said. "You
jinxing me."

"You don't need no jinx," Tiffany said. "You always
fishing in the wrong hole."

Uncle Frank got a strange look on his face then
chuckled. Miss Tiffany winked at him.

"What y'all taking about?" Cecil asked.

"Grown folks talk," Miss Tiffany said. She ambled to
the counter and opened the Tom's Food container. She
took out a cookie and gave it to Cecil.

"For you," she said. She turned to Uncle Frank.

"Now what you want?" she asked.

"Two boxes of wigglers, and one box of night crawlers."

"No minnows?"

Uncle Frank shook his head.

"Naw. They don't like minnows where we going."

"Y'all must be going to Church Lake."

"Yes, ma'am."

Miss Tiffany shook her head as she went to the back of the store.

"Some folks just don't know how to give up."

"I had it once, I'll have it again," Uncle Frank said.

Tiffany came back with four boxes. The white boxes had wigglers; the brown boxes the nightcrawlers.

"Keep them nightcrawlers cool," Miss Tiffany said. "They don't' like the heat."

"You tell him that every time we come here," Uncle Frank said.

"Man, give me my five dollars and get out my store," Miss Tiffany said.

Uncle Frank reached into his right pocket and took out four crumbled dollars. He reached into his left pocket and took out four quarters.

Miss Tiffany bagged the worms, then put two cans of soda in the bag as well.

"On the house," she said.

Uncle Frank leaned over the counter and kissed Miss Tiffany on the cheek.

"You so sweet," he said.

"Just remember to call me this week," she said.

"I will."

"Bye, Miss Tiffany!" Cecil said as they walked out of the bait shop.

"Bye, little man! Don't catch them all!"

Cecil grinned. "I won't."

They set out on the way to Church Lake. Uncle Frank opened Cecil's soda for him.

"What you think about Miss Tiffany, Cecil?"

Cecil looked confused. "I don't know. She's an old lady."

Uncle Cecil laughed. "Don't let her hear you say that. Besides, she ain't old. She's younger than your mama."

"Mama's old, too," Cecil said.

"You better not let your mama hear you say that less you want a whupping."

Uncle Frank took a long pull from his soda.

"Now when we get to the lake, I'm going to set you up at the bream hole. You remember how to take them off the hook, right?"

"Yes, sir."

"Good. I'm going out on the boat."

Cecil frowned. "Why can't I go out on the boat?"

"One, you don't know how to swim. Two, you don't have a life jacket. Three, because I said so."

"But I can't catch bass at the bream hole," Cecil fussed.

"No, you can't," Uncle Frank said. "You ain't ready for the big leagues. You need a little bit more practice. But you'll be ready next year. Then Ol' Uncle Frank will show how to hook 'em and reel 'em in."

"Like you reeled in Ol' Hoss?"

Uncle Frank frowned and Cecil giggled.

"Oh, so you Flip Wilson now," Uncle Frank said. "Well, let me tell you something. Today is Ol' Hoss's last day breathing water. I got this new lure from Tom Mann's down in Eufaula that's gonna hypnotize her like a cobra to a flute."

Cecil didn't know what any of that meant, but if Uncle Frank believed it, he would try to believe it, too.

It was still morning when they reached Church Lake. A one-lane dirt road snaked a half a mile from Macon Road to it. It was actually a pond, a one-acre man-made lake that once belonged to the farmer who owned the surrounding land. The locals called it Church Lake because it rested at the bottom of the hill where Big Bethel AME Church stood. The lake officially belonged to the church, but the members didn't mind folks indulging in its bounty. Most came to catch bream, shellcrackers and catfish, but Uncle Frank and a few others came for the bass.

The road was rough and muddy from a recent rain. Cecil and Uncle Joe jostled about as they rolled over the ruts in the dirt road. They reached the corner of the lake where the bream congregated, and Uncle Frank stopped the truck. Cecil pushed his door wide and jumped out.

"Slow down, boy!" Uncle Frank said. "Them fish ain't going nowhere!"

Cecil ignored his uncle, running until he reached the trunk of the pine tree that had fallen into the lake two years ago. Its submerged canopy created the perfect cover for minnows and the perfect refuge for bream. Cecil opened the box of wigglers, digging into the mulch and pulling out a worm. He baited his hook then casted just beyond the submerged branches, hoping he wouldn't get snagged. He sat on the trunk, rested his chin on his hands, and waited.

"I'm gonna be out in the boat!" Uncle Frank called out.

"Okay!" Cecil shouted, his eyes focused on the red and white bobber suspending his baited hook just above the limbs where the bream hid. He heard a splash then looked up to see Uncle Frank settling into the old johnboat that no one claimed but everyone used when they wanted to fish in the deep water near the lake dam.

He watched Uncle Frank paddle out to the deep end. That's where the big fish lived.

Cecil heard a smaller plop. He looked for his bobber and it was gone. He grabbed his pole then snatched hard, setting the hook. His rod bent and the tip danced back and forth.

"I got one!" he shouted. "I got one!"

"Better reel it in before it gets tangled in them branches!" Uncle Frank shouted back.

Cecil cranked his Zebco 33 reel as fast as his small hands could manage, but the bream on the end of his line wasn't budging. It held its place for a full minute before slowly coming closer and closer to the bank. Cecil watched the fish zigzag, using its wide body to resist. Cecil kept the pressure on until the bream gave up, laying on its side as he dragged it to the bank. Cecil was careful how he gripped the struggling fish, making sure he had it firmly before taking out the hook. After dropping the bream into his fish basket, he washed his hands in the lake water, drying them on his jeans. He was just about to get another wiggler from the bait box when Uncle Frank hollered.

"Woo wee! Here we go!"

Uncle Frank was on his knees in the johnboat, turning the handle on his spinning reel as fast as he could. His rod bowed, his spool singing as 15lb test line was stripped from his reel.

"Is it Ol' Hoss?" Cecil shouted.

"Yezzir!" Uncle Frank shouted back.

Uncle Frank reeled and reeled, but Old Hoss didn't budge.

"C'mon up here, Miss Hoss!" he said. "You know you tired."

As if on cue, Uncle Frank's line fell slack.

"God dammit! She broke the line!"

Uncle Frank slammed his rod and reel on the bottom of the johnboat. He was in the middle of a cussing fit when his line jerked. His eyes lit up and he snatched the tackle off the bottom of the boat and began reeling again. "Oh, you trying to be slick," he said. "Swimming to the boat and trying to get me all tangled up. That ain't happening!"

Ol' Hoss was fast, but Uncle Frank was faster. He took up all the slack line and was putting the pressure on the fish again.

"I got you now!" he said. "I know I got you . . ."

Uncle Frank's line went tight and snapped with a sound like a broken guitar. His rod straightened and Uncle Frank stood frozen, staring into the water.

"She gone?" Cecil asked.

Uncle Frank glared at Cecil. He opened his mouth to answer but something bumped the boat.

"What the hell?"

A fin rose from under the water behind Uncle Frank. It was huge, bigger than the shark fins Cecil had seen on National Geographics. But it wasn't a shark fin. It resembled a bass dorsal fin; a huge spiked fin. The fin streaked toward the johnboat.

"Uncle Frank! Look out!"

Uncle Frank look puzzled until he saw the big fin coming at him like a torpedo.

"Aw hell naw!"

The huge fish rammed the johnboat. Uncle Frank pitched back, falling into the lake as the boat flipped on top of him. Cecil ran back and forth, helpless.

"Uncle Frank! Uncle Frank!" he yelled.

Uncle Frank's head broke the water surface, his eyes wide with fear. He swam for the bank, his thick arms flailing the water. Cecil watched him come closer, then saw the fin appear behind his uncle.

"Swim faster, Uncle Frank! Faster!"

Uncle Frank's eyes narrowed, his arms moving faster, his legs kicking behind him. The fin disappeared, replaced by the head and open maw of the largest bass Cecil had seen in his life.

"Uncle Frank!"

The fish's mouth hovered over Uncle Frank for a second then smashed against the surface. Uncle Frank disappeared in an explosion of water. Cecil fell back in shock. The water settled, small ripples undulating to the shore. Cecil stared where he last saw Uncle Frank, then scanned the entire lake, refusing to accept what he'd just seen.

"Uncle Frank? Uncle Frank!"

The water roiled, becoming more and more violent until a massive fish tail thrashed the surface. The churning water changed from clear to red; moments later Uncle Frank's head broke the surface. He gasped then swam hard until he reached the bank. Cecil rushed to help him, but his uncle was on the grass spitting up breakfast and lake water before Cecil could reach him. Uncle Frank rolled onto his back, breathing hard. Cecil looked out on the lake and saw the giant fish's body floating on the surface, reddish water spreading around it. Cecil looked back to Uncle Joe and saw the knife in his right hand.

Uncle Frank sat up then turned around. A smile came to his face.

"I guess that new lure worked," he said.

Cecil laughed and Uncle Frank joined him.

"Come on, let's get the hell out of here," he said.

Uncle Frank stood and Cecil ran up to him and hugged him.

"I thought you were dead!"

Uncle Frank rubbed Cecil's head. "I thought so, too. Never thought I'd see the inside of a bass. Don't think I want to again."

Uncle Frank and Cecil ambled to the truck.

"This is gonna stay between you and me, okay?"

Cecil nodded. "Okay."

Uncle Frank opened the passenger door and helped Cecil inside. He trotted over to the driver's side, jumped inside, started the old truck and sped away. Cecil looked back as Church Lake faded away. He didn't know everything, but he was certain of one thing. He was never going fishing again.

Lightning Bug Boy

"Diane! Girl, where are you?"

Diane Collins squatted near the roses in her yellow play dress and no shoes, watching the pretty butterfly open and close its colorful wings. She eased her fingers closer and closer, waiting for the right moment. John-John used to catch butterflies and chase her with them when she was little, but she was ten now and wasn't afraid of them anymore.

The yellow butterfly's wings closed. A wide grin came to Diane's face. She was about to catch her first butterfly.

"Diane!"

Diane screeched and fell back on her backside. She watched the butterfly flutter way, then she looked into Mama's angry eyes.

"Girl, I've been looking all over for you. Come on here and change your clothes. Your Aunt Viola will be here any minute."

Mama grabbed her hand then pulled Diane into her arms.

"I'm not a baby," Diane protested.

"Then stop acting like one. Out here catching bugs like your brother. You got better sense than that."

Mama marched to the back porch. Diane looked back over her shoulder. The butterfly flapped its paper-thin wings and flew into the next-door neighbor's yard, seeking sweeter rewards among the red azaleas.

"I'll catch you next time!" Diane said as Mama carried her into the house.

Mama carried her through the kitchen then into the hallway. Diane hugged Mama's neck when Mama took one arm away to knock on John-John's bedroom door.

"You dressed?"

"Yes, ma'am!" John-John called out.

"Open the door and let me see."

John-John opened the door. Mama scrunched up her face and Diane giggled. John-John scowled at her.

"What you laughing at, pencil head!" he said.

"She's laughing at how that shirt is too small," Mama said.

"But I like it!"

"Boy, put on the shirt I put out for you."

"But mama I . . ."

"Don't argue with me," Mama said. "And you better not slam that door."

John-John mumbled a reply.

"Always trying to act up when his Daddy ain't here," Mama said.

"I don't," Diane said.

"No, you don't," Mama replied. "You act up all the time."

A car horn honked. Mama pushed John-John back into his room.

"Get dressed right now," she said.

Mama went back into the kitchen, Diane still on her shoulders. Aunt Viola walked in, wearing her jeans, tennis shoes and flannel shirt.

"Dot, I told you about leaving your back door unlocked," she said. "Anybody could walk in here."

"It's my back door," Mama said. "And how you know I don't want anybody walking in here?"

Mama and Aunt Viola laughed, and Diane laughed with them. Their joyful voices tickled her inside. Diane wished she had a sister like Aunt Viola, not a stupid brother.

John-John trudged out of his room and into the kitchen. Aunt Viola's smile brightened.

"Hey Jay Jay!"

John-John forced a smile to his face. "Hey, auntie."

"Y'all come on now," Aunt Viola said. "We got a long way to go."

"When y'all coming back?" Mama asked.

"It's gonna be late," Aunt Viola answered. "Probably after dark."

"You make sure you feed them," Mama said. "Don't be bringing no hungry children back to my house."

"Now you know better than that," Aunt Viola said.

"I sure do. That's why I told you."

Aunt Viola took Diane and John-John's hands then let them toward the door.

"You so hateful," she said to mama.

"Yeah, but I still love you."

Diane waved at mama as she stepped outside. John-John pouted.

Aunt Viola rushed to her car.

"Hold up, babies," she said. "Auntie has to move some things around."

Diane skipped in a circle while Aunt Viola cleared out her back seat, dropping the collection of textbooks and loose papers into the trunk of her Buick. John-John sat on the back steps pouting the entire time.

"Come on, babies!" Aunt Viola said.

Diane skipped to the car then tumbled inside, giggling as she rolled across the bench seat. John-John rose slowly from the stairs and death marched to the car, barely reaching it before falling inside, his legs hanging out.

"Lord, this child," Aunt Viola said. "I'm gonna give you an Oscar for that performance."

Diane saw a grin come to his face as Aunt Viola lifted his feet and pushed him the rest of the way into the car.

Diane raised her arms and Aunt Viola buckled her in. She then propped John-John up into a sitting position then strapped him in. Mama came to the screen door and waved goodbye as they backed out of the driveway into the street.

Aunt Viola sped through the neighborhood then onto the main road leading to the highway. Diane hung on the edge of her window, watching the world zoom by.

"What you looking at?" John-John said.

"Everything!" Diane replied.

"You act like you never seen outside before."

Diane ignored him. He was always fussing about something unless he was eating candy.

They exited the highway onto a two-lane road bordered by forest. The pine trees stood equal height and distance, planted forests that would one day fall to a pulpwooder's saw blade. But Diane didn't care. To her, it was a mystery waiting to be explored, a place full of rabbits to chase and butterflies to catch.

"Oh my goodness!" Aunt Viola said. "Look!"

Diane and John-John almost bumped heads as they leaned to the center of the back seat so they could see out the windshield. Four deer sprinted across the road, Aunt Viola slowing down to let them pass. As she sped up a straggler sprinted out onto the asphalt. Diane lunged forward and Aunt Viola screamed as she slammed on the brakes. The deer looked in their direction then jumped straight into the air. The car passed under the deer; Diane looked out the back window and saw the deer land on its hooves then run into the woods.

Aunt Viola pulled to the side of the road then climbed out of the car. She opened the passenger door on John-John's side and stuck her head inside, her face wrinkled with worry.

"Y'all okay?"

Diane and John-John nodded.

"I didn't know deer could fly," John-John said.

"They can't," Aunt Viola said. "But thank God they can jump. I owe too much on this car."

Diane clapped. This was already an adventure. John-John glared at her.

"What you happy about? We almost had a wreck!"

"Leave Diane alone," Aunt Viola said.

John-John fell back into his seat, his little arms folded across his chest.

"I hate this trip," he said.

Aunt Viola glanced into the back seat.

"What did you say? You talking back to me?"

"No."

"No what?"

"No, ma'am."

"Alright then."

Aunt Viola drove a few more miles until they reached the Little Uchee Creek Girl Scout camp. She took a right onto the hard pack dirt road, navigating the car through the winding turns and between the horse stables until they reached the lodge house. Diane's heart pattered as they came to a stop. So many woods to explore! There had to be a million butterflies in them, and she was going to catch every last one of them.

She was unbuckling her seatbelt before Aunt Viola reached the door. It swung wide and she jumped out, running toward the forest.

"Girl, wait!" Aunt Viola shouted.

Diane stopped so suddenly she almost fell. Aunt Viola opened John-John's door then waited.

"Come on, boy," she said. "Get out the car."

"I don't want to," John-John said.

Aunt Viola sighed, rolled her eyes then pulled John-John out the car.

"I should have left you at the house with your mama," she said. "Now go over to the playground with your sister."

"How long we gonna be here?" he asked.

"Long enough," Aunt Viola said. "I have a few things to take care of, then I'll take y'all to Krystals on the way back home."

John-John straightened and smiled. "Okay."

Diane giggled. Krystals was John-John's most favorite restaurant in the whole wide world. Hers, too.

"Now go play with your sister."

John-John trotted up to Diane.

"Race you!"

They sprinted to the swing set. John-John won, but he was older than her. One day she was going to beat him, she thought. They climbed into the swings, both trying to see which one could swing the highest. Diane looked out to the woods and saw butterflies fluttering among the wildflowers. She dragged her feet against the ground until her swing was low enough for her to jump out.

"Let's catch butterflies!" she said.

John-John ignored her, moving his legs in and out to increase his altitude. Diane skipped to the woods edge, her eyes focused on the flittering bugs. Unlike at home, she chased them, following them deeper into the field and closer to the woods. Then she saw a flash of light and her smile became even wider.

"Lightning bugs!"

She ran toward the glow, her hands open. The bugs increased to two, then five, then so many she couldn't count. Diane had never seen so many lightning bugs in her life. Their yellow-green brightness touched everything around them. The insects surrounded her, and she danced, humming a tune as she twirled around. The bugs

112

seem to dance with her, swirling in time, a few landing on her head and arms then flying away.

The lightning bugs drifted deeper into the pines and Diane followed. The further they went into the woods, the more numerous the bugs became. Soon there were so many Diane had to shade her eyes. The bugs formed a large flickering sphere, its pulse almost hypnotic. Diane was mesmerized. Then, without warning, they dispersed. It took Diane's eyes a moment to adjust, but when they did, what she saw startled her. A boy stood before her. He wore dirty coveralls, his hair matted on his head. His eyes and teeth radiated like the lightning bugs. Diane backed away as he smiled.

"Hey. My name is Bobby. What's yours?"

"Diane."

She took a step backwards. Bobby didn't move; he stood still, smiling at her.

"Do you want to play?" he asked.

Diane took another step back.

"Uh uh."

"Are you scared of me?"

Diane nodded.

Bobby smiled wider. "Don't be. I can bring the lightning bugs back."

Diane stopped.

"No, you can't."

"Yes, I can."

Diane folded her arms. "Do it."

Bobby closed his eyes. His fingers rolled into fists and wrinkles formed on his forehead. A minute later a lightning bug appeared, then another. Soon they swarmed around and between the children. Diane clapped her hands.

"Yay!"

Bobby opened his eyes.

"I can show you where there are a lot more."

He walked away, the lightning bugs following him. Diane looked back to the playground. John-John was still swinging. She glanced at the lodge. The lights were visible through the windows, and she could see Aunt Viola and the other ladies talking. The sun was setting, the last rays of light cutting through the trees.

"Okay," Diane said.

She followed Bobby into the woods. They travelled a trail, the lightning bugs illuminating the way. The path ended at a creek filled with granite rocks. There was a large rock near the bank; Bobby climbed it then sat.

"Come on up!" he said.

Diane tried to climb but couldn't get a good grip.

"I can't!" she said.

Bobby reached down. Diane touched his hand then drew way. It was cold like ice.

"I think I better go," Diane said.

"Wait," Bobby said. "You haven't seen everything."

Bobby closed his eyes again and clapped his hands. Frogs and crickets began chirping as if on cue, and the forest came alive in light. Lightning bugs filled the air. Lizards, frogs, and creatures Diane had never seen before crawled through the bushes, adding their brightness to the show. Even the creek seemed to glow. Diane neared the water's edge and spied tiny fish swimming along the bank, their backs shimmering. She looked back to Bobby who sat on the rock like a king on a throne.

"Why do they come to you?" she asked.

"Because they like me," Bobby said.

"Why?"

Bobby's face sagged. "Because they helped me when I was alone. They stayed with me until I went to sleep. So now I stay with them."

"Where are your mama and daddy?" Diane asked.

Bobby's face turned grim. "I don't know."

The light disappeared. The lightning bugs, frogs, fish; everything was gone. The only light remaining emanated from Bobby's eyes.

"Go away," he said. "I don't like you anymore."

Bobby closed his eyes and disappeared.

"Bobby?" Diane said. "Bobby!"

Diane fell to the ground and cried. She was alone in the wood in pitch blackness. There was no way she could find her way back.

"Diane!"

Diane sat up, wiping the tears from her eyes.

"Auntie!"

"Diane! Where are you baby?"

Diane jumped to her feet.

"I'm here Auntie! I'm here!"

Diane took a few steps then stopped. It was too dark for her to see where she was going, even if she tried to follow Aunt Viola's voice. She was about to start crying again when a lightning bug appeared before her.

"Go away!" she shouted. "Go away!"

Another bug appeared. They hovered about her head, and she tried to hit them, swinging as hard as she could. With every swipe, another lightning bug appeared. Soon a swarm danced around her.

"GO. AWAY!" Diane cried.

The bugs drifted away. Diane was so furious she chased them, trying her best to swat each one.

"Diane!"

Diane stopped. Her aunt sounded closer. The bugs stopped too, then continued flying away. Diane followed them, her anger subsiding.

"Diane? Baby?"

Auntie Viola's voice was louder.

"Diane!"

Diane's eyes went wide.

"John-John!"

"Auntie! I think she's over here!"

The bugs flew toward the voices and Diane followed. She smiled as the window lights of the lodge appeared in the distance.

"Auntie! John-John!"

"There she is!" an unfamiliar voice called out.

Diane saw bouncing light coming her way. As the light became brighter the lightning bugs dispersed, hiding their radiance and disappearing into the darkness. Aunt Viola was the first person to reach her. She dropped her flashlight and swept Diane up into her arms.

"Thank you, Jesus!" she shouted.

Diane hugged Aunt Viola tight.

"It's okay, auntie," she said. "I'm alright."

She felt a tug on her foot then looked down into John-John's smug face.

"You in trouble," he said.

"Hush now," Aunt Viola said. She carried Diane back to the lodge.

"Girl, what are you doing in these woods by yourself? Didn't I tell you to stay at the playground?"

"I saw the butterflies," Diane said. "And then I saw lightning bugs. A whole lot of them. And then I saw the lightning bug boy."

Aunt Viola stopped walking. "You saw who?"

"The lightning bug boy," Diane repeated. "His name is Bobby, and he made the bugs come."

Another woman approached, tall with light skin wearing cat eyeglasses.

"What did you say that boy's name was?"

"Bobby."

"Oh my God," the woman said. "Y'all come inside."

Aunt Viola carried Diane inside the lodge. The other women crowded around them as they entered.

"I called the police," one of them said. "I guess we don't need them now."

"Yes, we do," the woman with the cat-eye glasses said. "Barbara, can you sit out here with the children? I need to talk to Viola."

Barbara nodded. Aunt Viola put Diane down.

"I'll be right back, baby. Miss Barbara is going to watch y'all for a minute."

"I'm hungry," Diane said.

"Me, too!" John-John said.

"I'll fix y'all something," Barbara said. "Y'all want a hot dog?"

"I want Krystals!" John-John said.

"Y'all gonna have to be happy with what we have," Miss Barbara said.

Diane and John-John waited for the hot dogs. Diane crept to the door of the room where Aunt Viola and the other lady went. She couldn't hear what they said, but she could tell it was some serious grown folks talk. After a few minutes, she heard Aunt Viola say mama's name.

"Hot dogs are ready!" Miss Barbara announced.

Diane's stomach growled as she ambled over to Miss Barbara. She joined John-John at the small table, and they ate as the adults whispered. Diane was finishing her second hot dog when she saw flashing lights outside of the lodge. But these were not lightning bugs lights. These lights were red and blue.

"It's the police!" John-John shouted.

He jumped from his seat then rushed to the window.

"Sit back down, boy," Aunt Viola said.

"But I want to see!"

"You've seen enough."

Aunt Viola walked to John-John, grasped his shoulders then guided him back to his seat.

"Now you sit right here and don't get up until I tell you to," she said. "If you don't, I'm telling your mama how bad you were."

John-John dropped his elbows on the table and his chin into his palms. Moments later there was a knock on the door. The lady with the cat eyeglasses answered.

"Come in, officers," she said. "I'm Miss Clayborn. Right this way."

The officers came inside. They all looked at Diane and walked toward her.

"Uh oh!" John-John said. "They coming to arrest you!"

"No, they ain't!" Diane squealed.

"Calm down," Aunt Viola said. "They're here to ask you some questions about that boy you met in the woods."

One of the officers, a tall brown man with a gentle smile, took off his hat then knelt down until his face was even with Diane's.

"What's your name?" he asked.

"Diane Jones."

"I'm Sam Price," the officer said. "Your auntie and Miss Clayborn said you met a boy in the woods."

Diane nodded her head.

"What was his name," Officer Price asked.

"His name was Bobby."

The officer took a notepad and pen out of his top pocket."

"Did he say his last name?"

"No."

The officer's smiled dimmed.

"You sure?"

"Yes, sir."

"Diane, can you show me where you last saw Bobby?"

Diane shook her head.

"Why?"

"Because it's dark."

"I don't think she needs to go back into those woods," Aunt Viola said.

"We've been looking for Bobby for a long time," Officer Sam said. "The sooner we find him, the better."

Officer Sam turned his attention back to Diane,

"Diane, Officer Simmons and I would like you to show us where you and Bobby went. We'll have our flashlights, and your Aunt Viola will be with us, too."

"What?" Aunt Viola said. "I ain't said nothing about going into them woods at night!"

"Please, ma'am," Officer Sam said. "We need your help."

"Can I go?" John-John asked.

"No," Aunt Viola said. "You're staying right here."

"Okay then," Officer Sam said. "You ready, Diane?"

Diane extended her arms. Officer Sam smiled then picked her up.

The officer carried Diane outside; Officer Simmons and Aunt Viola held the flashlights.

"Okay, Diane, which way?"

Diane was confused for a moment until she saw a lightning bug flashing brighter than she'd ever seen. She pointed at the bug.

"That way," she said.

Officer Sam entered the woods, his flashlight pointed ahead. Despite its strength Diane could still see the lightning bug, its flickering leading the way. Eventually they heard the gurgling of the creek.

"We're almost there," Diane said.

They continued until the flashlight illuminated the large rock that Bobby sat on.

"Here," Diane said.

Officer Sam placed her down. Aunt Viola moved forward then stood beside her. Officer Sam motioned with his head and he and Officer Simmons began searching the area.

"Sam," Officer Simmons said. "Take a look at this."

Officer Sam jogged to where his partner stood. They talked for a moment, then Officer Sam came to Diane and Aunt Viola.

"You did a good job, Diane," he said. "We're going back to the lodge now."

"Are we finished?" Aunt Viola asked. "Because I need to get these children back to their mama. She's probably worried sick."

"Yes, ma'am, we are," Officer Sam said. "You might want to keep the children away from the television for a few days."

The grownups were quiet as they walked back to the lodge. Aunt Viola took Diane back to the table where John-John still sat. The grownups gathered around the police officers, talking low so Diane and John-John couldn't hear them.

"What did y'all do?" John-John asked.

"Nothing," Diane replied. "I showed them where Bobby took me."

John-John frowned. "How did you know? It was dark."

"A lightning bug showed me."

"You lying."

"No, I'm not!"

Their brewing argument was stifled by a loud moan. Miss Clayborn stumbled to the nearest chair, took off her glasses and sat. She was crying. Aunt Viola came to the table, her eyes glistening.

"Come on, babies," she said. "Time to go home."

The ride home was tense and silent. Mama and daddy were waiting when they arrived, peering through the screen door. She marched down the stairs right up to the car.

"Viola, where y'all been?"

Aunt Viola gave mama a look.

"Let's get the children inside first," she said. "I'll tell you everything."

Diane and John-John hugged mama then followed her inside. They took their baths, brushed their teeth then lay in their beds, straining to listen to mama and Aunt Viola talk. Not long after, their bedroom door opened, and they both pretended to be asleep. Mama and Aunt Viola hugged and kissed them both, then left the room.

* * *

Mama wouldn't let them watch TV for a week. They continued their summer routine, playing all day and eating as much as mama would let them. One day, Diane was visiting her friend Christine. The two were playing in Christine's room when Diane overheard Christine's parents talking.

"I'm so glad they found that boy's body," her mama said.

"Me, too," her daddy said. "I mean, I wish they'd found him alive, but at least they get to put him to rest."

"I wonder what happened?" her mama said.

"They don't know," her daddy replied. "The body was too decomposed for them to tell. And to imagine they looked all over the place for him, and his body was right beside that rock."

Diane's eyes went wide, and she stopped playing. "Didn't you know his parents?" her daddy asked. "I know his mama," her mother said. "Louise was always talking about Bobby. The day he disappeared I thought she was going to die. I guess a part of her did." Tears came to Diane's eyes, and she sobbed.

"Diane? What's wrong?" Christine asked.

"I want to go home," she said.

Christine's parents took her home. It was dark when they arrived; when Diane saw mama she ran to her, jumping into her arms.

"What's wrong, baby?" mama asked.

"Nothing," Diane replied. "I just wanted to come home."

"Let's go inside," mama said. "I'll fix you some ice cream."

Mama walked to the door. Diane gazed over her shoulder, watching Christine and her parents drive away. A glimmer caught her eye and she looked to the old oak tree in their back yard. Under its canopy the lightning bugs danced, their light brighter than she'd ever seen. A warmth grew in her chest.

"Hi, Bobby," she whispered. "Bye, Bobby."

By the time she entered the house with mama, she smiled.

Miss Berry's Boy

Some folks just mean for no reason. They come out the womb raising hell and go to the grave the same way. Ain't nobody done nothing to them to make them that way. They just got the devil in them. That was Miss Berry's boy.

It was a shame, actually. Louise Berry was the sweetest woman God ever put on this earth. The woman would break her back to do for anybody, white or black. Some folks say that's why she had a baby like Rufus. Miss Berry had to be his mama. Anybody else would have killed him in his sleep.

Rufus was a bad boy from the day he was born. Almost killed Louise at birth. The midwife had to use all her skills and herbs to bring that boy into the world and keep both him and his mama alive. When she spanked that boy's bottom, he wailed like a haint, shaking that old midwife to the bone. She took off out of Miss Berry's shack like she was on fire and never came back.

The only time that boy was calm was when he was in his mama's arms. That was bad, because Miss Berry's husband, Nathan Berry, was a good colored man. He worked hard in them cotton fields during the week, never went out drinking at the juke joint by Uchee Creek at night, and was always at church every Sunday, sitting on the front pew of Big Bethel AME Zion Church in his Sunday best beside Louise. But that boy hated his daddy. He wouldn't let Nathan touch him. If he pointed at Rufus he'd get to hollerin' like somebody stabbed him with an ice pick. Got so bad that one day Nathan told Louise it was either him or Rufus. Now anybody with any kind of common sense knows good and damn well that a woman ain't gonna choose a man over her child, no matter how evil that child or how good that man. So Nathan packed his bags, climbed onto his red mule and left the county.

Nathan left Louise in a bad way. She couldn't get a job because wasn't nobody in their right mind gonna let that boy in their house. So she took to washing and cooking to make ends meet. Thank the good Lord she was good at both. Louise used what little money she saved up to get her a cow and a few chickens. She planted collards, mustard greens, black eyed peas and lima beans. Every morning she would rise before the sun and start cooking. By daybreak she was on the side of the road with breakfast for the men going to work on the local farms. She would carry that boy around on her hip the whole time, and he would give the evil eye to each one of them. God ain't made another woman as good as Louise Berry, and he never will.

Time finally come for Rufus Berry to go to school. Louise dressed him in a white shirt and brand-new coveralls with the best secondhand shoes she could find. She made a sack lunch for him, kissed him on his forehead then walked with him for two miles to the schoolhouse. Miss Turnipseed, the teacher, waited outside, her smile fading when she saw Louise and that boy. She'd heard the rumors; everybody in the county had. But Miss Turnipseed wasn't no pushover. Ever since she'd come to the county from Atlanta after graduating from Morris Brown College, she'd run the colored schoolhouse with kindness and a firm hand. She wasn't about to let no five-year-old wild child run over her. That's what she thought. Old Miss Seed didn't make it a day and a half. She marched Rufus back home, looking like she was holding hands with a hornet. Soon as he saw his house, that boy calmed down like a puppy. Miss Turnipseed banged on the door until Louise opened it, flour from her latest batch of pies on her apron, hands, and cheeks.

"Here," Miss Turnipseed said, shoving Rufus into his house. "Don't you ever bring this boy back to my schoolhouse again!"

"But he needs an education!" Louise replied.

Miss Turnipseed looked thoughtful for a moment, then her eyes brightened.

"I tell you what. I'll bring you everything you need to teach him yourself. When he's ready, I'll test him, but only with you present."

"I got too much to do to school him," Louise said. "I ain't got the time."

"Well, you gonna have to make the time," Miss Turnipseed said. "Because if you bring that boy back to my school, one of us is gonna end up dead, and I'm determined it ain't gonna be me!"

So that's how Rufus got to be homeschooled.

Miss Louise couldn't teach Rufus and get chores done at the same time, so she put that boy to work. There was field work before sunrise, lessons in the morning, more farm work in the afternoon, woodchopping at dusk, then lessons after dinner. Miss Turnipseed kept her promise, bringing assignments by and testing Rufus when it was time. That's when Miss Louise and Miss Turnipseed discovered Rufus was as smart as he was mean.

Rufus's body grew with his mind. By the time he was twelve that boy stood over six feet all, all arms and legs and a big ol' head. It was then that girls took to noticing Rufus, because not only was he tall, he was a handsome thing, too. Folks that remembered his daddy said he was the spitting image of him. Miss Louise found herself working overtime, especially in the summer, keeping girls (and some women) away from Rufus and keeping him away from them.

While most boys back then stopped schooling around thirteen, Miss Turnipseed kept bringing lessons and

Rufus kept learning, except now he was smelling himself and became too hard for Miss Louise to handle. The boy kept doing his chores, but there were only so many hours in the day. Rufus took to gambling, fighting and whoring, building a bad reputation among colored folks and white folks. Problem was, everybody was scared of him, even the sheriff. By the time he was eighteen, Rufus Berry was 250 pounds of country boy muscle and spitfire. Nobody could beat him at cards, drinking or scrappin'.

Relief came to the county with the Great War. Rufus decided he would enlist. It was a steady job, and he could fight white folks without getting in trouble. He packed what little possessions he had, kissed Miss Louise goodbye, then walked to the train station where he spent his gambling money on a one-way ticket to Harlem. When he got there, he was a sight to see, standing out like a goose at a chicken dance. A few of them city boys started to make fun of him, but after a few broken jaws and lost teeth, they stopped. Rufus enlisted in the 369th, also known as the Harlem Hellfighters. After intense training, he and the other Negro soldiers shipped out to France.

If there was ever a man made for war, it was Rufus Berry. All those years of fighting trained him for that moment, and all the hard work on the farm made him tougher than barbed wire. And the French loved him. Rufus discovered that there was a place where white folks respected Negroes, well, at least more than them rednecks down South. The French army gave them awards despite the protest of the American officers. It was so good that after the war, Rufus stayed for a time in France. He made a good living as a bouncer and a nightclub manager. After a while Rufus got tired of France and returned home. Well, almost. He followed his army buddies back to New York City, where his brain and his brawn earned him a pretty penny. All the while Rufus sent letters home to his mama letting her know how he was doing, and he always included a few dollars to help her with the farm. He probably would have stayed in the big city, but Rufus's life was about to go through the worst change ever. On a cold December afternoon, he got a letter from home telling him his mama was sick. Without hesitation Rufus jumped in his car and headed back south to Clayborn County.

The day Rufus came home was a day to remember. He arrived driving a '28 Nash coupe, speeding down Highway 216. Now everybody knew that road was a speed trap except for Rufus, seeing that he'd been gone for a while. No sooner did he pass a stand of red oaks at Bullard Road did county deputy Calhoun Bodeen speed out of hiding, siren blaring. Rufus pulled over, cussing under his breath. Calhoun swaggered to the driver's side and received a double shock. Not only was there a Negro sitting at the steering wheel, that Negro was none other than Rufus Berry.

"Calhoun, is that you?" Rufus said.

Calhoun was speechless. He'd received a good whupping or three from Rufus before coming to his senses and leaving well enough alone. He calmed down and a grin formed on his ruddy face. Times were different now. He was an officer of the law and a member of good standing with the Klan. He stood a little straighter as he gripped his gun belt with both hands.

"Welcome home, Rufus," he said, trying to make his voice sound deeper than it was. "Heard about your mama."

"Thank you, Calhoun," Rufus said. "Now can you tell me what this is all about?"

"Caught you speeding," Calhoun said.

"I don't see how you did that, seeing that there's no speed limit sign on this road."

Calhoun's eyes narrowed. "You calling me a liar, Rufus?"

"No, just making an observation."

Calhoun stepped away from the car, his hand moving toward his revolver. "No, what?" he said.

Rufus looked confused for a moment then a smirk came to his face. He reached into his back seat then stepped out his car with a Tommy Gun.

"You musta forgot who I am," Rufus said.

Calhoun swallowed.

"I ain't come down here for no trouble, but I ain't running from it," Rufus continued. "I'm here to see about my mama, and I'll be here until she's gone to Glory. I heard what y'all been doing down here, but I'll be damned after serving this country in the war that I'm gonna let y'all backwood crackers get the best of me. Now how much I owe you?"

"Wha . . . what?" Calhoun said.

"How much I owe you for the ticket?"

"Um . . . twenty dollars?" Calhoun answered.

Rufus reached into a pant pocket with his left hand, took out a twenty-dollar bill, and handed it to Calhoun. The rattled deputy took the money then stuffed it into his pocket. Calhoun nodded then backed away to his patrol car. He jumped in, started it, did a quick u-turn and sped away, Rufus watching him until he drove out of sight.

Calhoun told Sheriff Luther Coleman what happened between him and Rufus and Luther blew up like a bad moonshine still. Luther knew all about Rufus, but he wasn't about to let no colored man walk around Clayborn County like he was untouchable. As sheriff and a well-respected member of the local Klan, he would not tolerate it. However, there was the situation of Miss Louise. Local folks loved Rufus's mama more than they hated him, so Luther made a decision. He would look the other way on Rufus's disrespect until Miss Louise passed away, which according to Dr. Sizemore, wasn't too long coming.

"You keep an eye on that boy," Luther said to Calhoun. "Let him know we watching him."

When Rufus finally arrived at his mama's house he ran straight up the porch stairs, through the screen door and to his mama's room. Miss Louise was sicker than she let on, but when her baby boy came home, she let herself fall into his attention. Rufus took care of her just like she took care of him when he was a terrible baby boy. He cooked, cleaned, washed, and kept up the farm. A lot of folks dropped by to help out, but he wouldn't let anybody inside that house unless Miss Louise requested them. At night, after his mama was fast asleep, Rufus would sit in the old rocking chair on the front porch with a pipe and a bottle of whiskey, sipping and smoking until he fell asleep.

Every Sunday Rufus drove Miss Louise to church in his fancy car, carrying her into and out the church like she was a newborn baby. He was so gentle with her, that some folks thought Rufus might have changed for the better. But they were wrong. Dead wrong.

Calhoun took the sheriff's words to heart. Every day, right around sundown, he would cruise by the farm. Rufus would be sitting on the front porch, a smoldering cigar in one hand, a jar of whisky in the other, taking the time to rest after tending to his mama. A smirk would come to his face as he watched Calhoun drive by. He'd raise his glass and nod his head; Calhoun would scowl and keep on driving.

The longer Rufus stayed, the more worried the colored folks got. The elders thought his presence would rile up the Klan and they would all pay for it. As much as they liked what he was doing for Miss Louise, Rufus had to go. But everybody was too scared to ask him to leave. Well, almost everybody.

Rufus was sitting on his mama's porch 'round evening time like always, waiting for Calhoun to make his drive by. Instead, an old pickup truck and dusty sedan came rumbling up the road then stopped in front of the house. A delegation of prominent Negroes led by Reverend George Abraham Jones marched up the walkway then stopped at the stairs. Rufus rose from his rocking chair like a huge shadow pushed up by the sunrise.

"Reverend," he said.

Reverend Jones took off his hat then nodded.

"Rufus."

Rufus folded his thick arms across his wide chest.

"What brings y'all out this way? Y'all come to see mama?"

"How is Miss Louise?" the reverend asked.

Rufus's eyes dimmed. "As well as expected. Won't be long now."

Jimmy Adams, a tall, coal black man with teeth like sunshine, stepped up.

"How you know that?" he said, his voice trembling. Jimmy had been sweet on Miss Louise at one time, but he never took the time to let her know.

"I used to see that look all the time on boys about to meet their maker in the Great War," Rufus said.

Jimmy dropped his head with a step back, giving Reverend Jones the floor once again.

"Rufus, we know how much you love your mama. Ain't no greater love than a child for they mama. We appreciate you coming back to take care of her in her time of need. But the fact of the matter is that since you come home, certain white folks have been agitated."

"What white folks?" Rufus asked.

The reverend frowned. "You know what and who I'm talking about."

"Them crackers in the Klan!" Jimmy blurted out. The reverend's head snapped around to glare at Jimmy.

"We ain't using that kinda talk around here," The reverend said.

"Why not?" Rufus said. "We all know who runs this county."

"I'm not here to talk about that," the reverend said. "I'm here to talk about you. Your presence is putting the lives of respectable Negroes in jeopardy. But I believe there is a solution. If you were to leave as soon as possible, things would simmer down. We could get some of the wives to look after your mama, and we would inform you of her passing so you could come down and attend the funeral. Of course, you would have to leave before the repast."

Rufus sat down then picked up his cigar. He took his time lighting it, then took a long drag. He let the smoke out like cold molasses before he spoke.

"I ain't going no damn where, reverend," he said. "Except to make a telephone call."

Rufus went inside the house. He came back out with his car keys.

"I need y'all to do me a favor," he said. "Watch my mama till I get back."

Rufus walked through the confused men, hopped into his car, and drove away. As he was speeding down the road, he passed Deputy Calhoun, on his way to do his nightly drive by. Calhoun almost wrecked his patrol car making a u-turn to follow Rufus. He trailed Miss Berry's boy to McDaniel's General Store across the line into

Polk County. Calhoun had no authority there, and what was worse, Tommy McDaniel considered himself the colored man's friend. An attitude like that would normally get a white man's business burned to the ground, but most of the white and black folks in a five-county radius owed him money in some way, shape, or form. Rufus strode into the front door of the store and was greeted by Tommy's smiling pasty face.

"Rufus Berry!" Tommy bellowed. "I heard you was back!"

"How you doing, Tommy?" Rufus asked.

He and Tommy were shaking hands when Calhoun entered the store. Tommy looked over Rufus's shoulder and his smile faded.

"Calhoun," he said.

Calhoun took off his hat. "Mr. McDaniel."

"You lost boy?" Tommy asked. "I see a Clayborn County patrol car in my parking lot, and this ain't Clayborn County."

Calhoun scowled as he pushed his hat back.

"Now, Tommy, I know you ain't about to put this nigger ahead of a white man, are you?"

Tommy placed a friendly hand on Rufus's shoulder. "Excuse me, Rufus."

Tommy walked up to Calhoun and stood so close to him he could smell yesterday's dinner on his breath.

"This is my damn store, peckerwood, and I'll do what I damn well please. As a matter of fact, you best be getting out of here before Sheriff Don smells your ass."

"God dammit, Tommy!" Calhoun shouted. "You not just gonna . . . "

Tommy punched Calhoun straight in the gums. Calhoun fell on his ass, eyes wide and mouth bleeding.

"Get out of my store boy," Tommy said.

Calhoun got up on his feet while rubbing his jaw.

"You ain't heard the last of this!" he shouted between his fingers.

"You better hope I have," Tommy said.

Calhoun stomped out the store, jumped into his patrol car and made a storm of rock and dirt as he tore out of the parking lot.

"Damn fool," Tommy said. He turned to Rufus. "What you need?"

"I need you to make a call for me," Rufus said. He took a piece of paper out of his overall pocket then handed it to Tommy. Tommy read it; confusion took over his face.

"What's this all about?" he said.

"Nothing," Rufus said.

Tommy's eyes narrowed. "Be careful, Rufus. Don't get in no trouble."

"I ain't never careful," Rufus replied. "And I ain't scared of trouble."

Rufus waited until Tommy made the call to his satisfaction. He thanked his old friend by buying ten dollars' worth of groceries and other items before leaving the store and returning home. The pastors were still there, praying over Miss Louise like she was about to die any minute. She looked at Rufus as he entered and sighed with relief.

"Y'all git," he said.

The pastors scattered like water bugs, jumping back into their car and speeding away.

"Don't ever leave me alone with them leeches ever again," Miss Louise said.

"I won't," Rufus replied. "Next time you see them will be in Heaven."

About two weeks after Tommy made that call for Rufus, Calhoun saw a strange sight from behind the Coca Cola billboard on Highway 27. Three trucks full of colored men cruised by him well within the speed limit, but that didn't stop Calhoun. He followed the caravan through the county, and his eyes went wide when each one of them pulled onto the dirt road leading to Miss Berry's farm. The trucks honked their horns and moments later Rufus appeared on the front porch, an unlit cigar in his hand, a big broad smile on his face. He greeted each man with a hug and a pat on the back, then they began unloading their trucks and setting up military style tents on the property. Calhoun sped down the road to the sheriff's office, telling Luther between gasps what he'd just seen. Luther wasted no time gathering all his deputies and a few deputized men then speeding to the farm. By the time they arrived the black men were scattered around the property doing various chores. The sheriff's convoy eased up the dirt road, parking in front of the house. Rufus sat on the porch, his cigar lit, conversing with one a heavy light-skinned man. As the sheriff sauntered up to the porch, he noticed every last one of the men had stopped whatever they were doing to glare at the sheriff and his men. The sheriff also noticed something else: every man had a pistol in his pocket. Rufus stepped off the porch and met the sheriff in the road.

"What you want, sheriff?" Rufus asked.

Luther spread his chest. "What the hell is going on here, boy? Where all these niggers come from?"

Rufus took a moment to control his temper before answering.

"These men—" his voice rose when he said men— "are my army buddies from New York. They come down to help me manage things."

"You couldn't find no local boys to do it?"

"Didn't want 'em," Rufus said. "This is hard work. I needed men like me. Men who been off to war. Men that ain't afraid of nothing."

The two fell silent, staring at each other like two roosters in a cock fight.

"How long your 'friends' planning on being here?" Luther asked.

"Until it's time for me to go," Rufus answered.

"Which from the look of things, won't be long now." Luther gripped his gun belt. "Just what are you trying to prove, boy?"

"I ain't got nothing to prove," Rufus said. "I'm here trying to enjoy with my mama whatever time she's got left. Looks like to me you the one trying to prove something."

"If I see one of them Yankee nigras off your property, they're going to jail," Luther promised. "You hear me?"

Rufus smirked. "I hear you. Now if you'll excuse me, it's mama's supper time."

Rufus walked away, his men keeping an eye on the sheriff and deputies until he nodded as he entered the house. They went back to their chores.

Luther spun around and stomped back to his car. This was getting out of hand. He needed more help, and he knew just who to call.

Two weeks after Rufus's friends arrived, the day he dreaded came to pass. Miss Louise died. She passed away as Rufus read her favorite Bible passage, holding his hand with her ever-present smile on her ageless face. Rufus let out a wail that could be heard for two miles, a sound so sad that every hound dog in the range of his sadness joined his mournful cry. Despite the sheriff's warning, he sent his friends to inform everyone she knew, which was most of the county. People visited the house endlessly while Rufus fought his grief to make arrangements for her funeral. The wake was held in the parlor of Jones Funeral Home, the local Negro mortician whose family had served the colored community for almost one hundred years. Malcolm Jones, the latest patriarch of the clan, wanted to have two viewings, one for Negroes and another for white folks. But Rufus wasn't having it.

"Mama ain't make no difference between white folks and Negroes. If they can't see her like she'd want 'em to, then the Hell with 'em."

Miss Louise's wake was the first time anybody could remember that white folks and Negroes in the county did something together. It was repeated the next day at her funeral. It was standing room only in Mount Olive Baptist Church. Rufus sat on the front pew, comforted by relatives he barely knew, while the choir sang mama's favorite hymns. Folks were asked to drop notes in a basket expressing their sentiments because there were too many people who wanted to share their love for Miss Louise. Reverend Jones took the pulpit and delivered a eulogy that brought tears to the eyes of every single person in that little church. Rufus's friends served as pallbearers, carrying the small coffin to the cemetery in the back of the church to a grave dug under the branches of the huge white oak tree older than Georgia. The choir sang Miss Louise's favorite hymn, Amazing Grace, as her coffin was lowered into the red clay and the world saw Louise Berry for the last time on this side of Glory.

It didn't take long for the sheriff to hatch his plan to get rid of Rufus Berry once and for all. The call went out to every Klan member in a five-county area. They were all to meet Monday morning on the road in front of Miss Berry's house, ready to handle business. The deputies gathered the night before at the sheriff's house for a hearty meal and preparation to show colored folks and white folks once and for all who controlled Clayborn County.

The sheriff's local militia woke with the rising sun, loaded their pistols, hunting rifles and shotguns and climbed in their pickup trucks and cars ready to deliver righteous justice. Reverend Robert 'Billy Boy' Preston said a prayer for them and to their success. The caravan was a grand sight, rolling down Highway 27 with lights on despite the cloudless sunny day. Sheriff Coleman led the procession, Deputy Calhoun brought up the rear, with various trucks and cars packed with local Klansmen in between.

As the Berry home came into view, Luther grinned like a happy gator. The tents were gone. The sheriff suspected Rufus and his gang had high-tailed it out of the county overnight. But he was wrong. The caravan came closer, and the sheriff's face transformed from joy to dread. Rufus's friends stood in front of the house, dressed in the suits they wore to Miss Berry's funeral. But instead of holding programs and Bibles, they held Tommy guns, Browning rifles and shotguns.

"What in the Hell?" he whispered.

The caravan halted before the house and the deputies and Klansmen reluctantly unloaded from their cars. Deputy Calhoun trotted up to the sheriff, his thin face tight with worry.

"Luther, we wasn't expecting this," he said. "Them niggers got guns. Lots of guns."

"I ain't blind, boy," Luther said.

Pete Bowman, wizard of the Toffee County KKK, waddled up to Luther, huffing from the short walk.

"Luther, you ain't tell us these nigras were gonna be armed," he said.

"I didn't know," Luther replied.

"Didn't you say Rufus fought in the war with the 369th?"

Luther looked at Pete. "Yeah. So what?"

"So I'm suspecting them boys with him are from the 369th, too."

"And?"

"We might want to reconsider this operation."

"Pete, you got something you need to tell me?"

"I served in the war, too," Pete said. "And I'm here to tell you that them boys with the 369th were something else. They fought with the French because we ain't want to have nothing to do with them. Them Frenchies gave them medals for bravery, and they deserved them. The Huns called them Hellfighters. Them boys ain't afraid of fighting, and they ain't afraid of killing."

Luther rubbed his chin. "Looks like negotiations might be in order."

"Sound like the smart choice," Pete said. "I got a family, and I want to see them after this is over."

Luther gripped his gun belt.

"Calhoun, come with me."

Calhoun's eyes went wide. "What?!"

"You heard me."

Luther addressed the rest of the men.

"Y'all stay put until you hear from me. Okay?"

The men nodded, some of them looking relieved.

Luther grabbed Calhoun's arm.

"Let's go."

Calhoun jerked his arm away then followed.

"I'm coming, but my mama is gonna be real mad if you get me shot."

Luther laughed. "You better hope that's all you get."

* * *

Rufus sat on the porch, watching Sheriff Jones and Calhoun walk up the dirt road to the house, their eyes darting from side to side. He positioned his men so they could lay effective crossfire against anyone trying to advance on the house, and he had a couple of men hidden at the edge of the woods with sniper rifles. He waited until the lawmen were halfway up the road before putting out his cigar, picking up his Tommy Gun, then stepping off the porch to meet them. He still wore the suit he buried his mama in, a red rose tucked in his top pocket. He stopped six feet from the sheriff.

"That's close enough," he said.

Sheriff Jones gripped his gun belt.

"What you trying to do, Rufus?"

Rufus tilted his hat with the barrel of his machine gun.

"I could ask you the same question, sheriff. All I did was come home to take care of my mama. You the one that made this a spectacle."

"Rufus, you know good and damn well you can't come down here acting like you own the place. Other colored folks might get ideas."

Rufus shrugged. "Ain't about to get into all that. I'm just talking to you about what you and these Klan boys think y'all about to do. You got us outnumbered, but we got you outgunned. And every last one of these men with me ain't scared of dying. That's the difference, sheriff. That's the reason I always been the way I've been. We all gonna die, either today or fifty years from now. And for a Negro, it's twice as bad. No matter when it happens, it's still the same thing."

Rufus's eyes didn't waver, and Luther was reminded why everybody in Clayborn County was afraid of him. The sheriff blinked before replying.

"I'ma let you and your boys go this time around," Luther said. "Get your things and get out of the county."

"You ain't letting us do a damn thing," Rufus said. "I'll tell you what's gonna happen. We are gonna leave.

139

Not because you want us to, but because I'm sick of this place. The only person that ever mattered to me was my mama, and she meant the world to me. And now she's gone. So, I'm gonna leave this shithole of a county, and you'll never see me again. And if you or your 'boys' try anything, more than half of you won't live to tell about it. And I'll make sure you'll be the first to lead the way to Hell."

Luther started to reach for his pistol, but Calhoun grabbed his hand. Luther tried to pull free, but Calhoun held him tight like a beaver trap.

"I ain't ready to die today, sheriff," Calhoun said.

Rufus grinned. "You smarter than him. Now y'all git."

Calhoun let Luther go. In Luther's mind Luther yanked free. Calhoun led back down the road, the sheriff walking backwards for a while before turning and stomping back to the others.

"They're leaving," Sheriff Luther said. "We'll stay here until they do."

Rufus called his men together. They packed their belongings, loaded their trucks, then drove single file down the dirt road from Miss Berry's house, onto Highway 25, then out of the county.

Rufus Berry was true to his word. Nobody ever saw him in the county again. But there were signs he was never far away. There was the grand tombstone delivered to the church one Monday morning all the way from Columbus, the biggest and most beautiful piece of granite in the county that lasted long after the church was abandoned. Then there were the fresh roses that always appeared on Miss Louise's grave on her birthday and Easter.

And the colored folks changed, too. They were less likely to look away, to accept bad deals for their crops, to stay silent when the county tried to pass unfavorable laws, and back down when the Klan tried to march down Main Street. The people never forgot Miss Berry; but most of all, *nobody* ever forgot Miss Berry's boy.

Muscadine Wine

"Dot, you ready?"

Dorothy 'Dot' Simpson shifted her hat from the left to the right, then frowned.

"I wish my head wasn't so big!" she said. She took off the hat then threw it on her bed.

"Girl, you still in here fussing with your clothes?"

Dot twisted around to see Sis standing in the door of their bedroom.

"I'm ready," she said.

"About time," Sis said. "Rock and them about to leave us."

Dot followed her younger sister down the hallway then out the back door to the steep stairs. The drum holding leftovers to feed the hogs reeked, but Dot was used to the smell. The farm wasn't the most floral place during the spring and summer, but it was home, and she loved it. Rock saw them descending the stairs and blew the horn, a mischievous grin on his face.

"Y'all hurry up!" he shouted.

"You see us coming!" Dot shouted back playfully. "Stop acting up." Sis opened the passenger door and popped in, sliding the bench seat to sit next to Rock. Dot got in and closed the door.

"You sit in the middle next time, Dot," Rock said. "Sis's hips too big."

"Johnny Turnipseed don't think so," Sis replied.

"Don't be nasty," Dot scolded.

"You sound like mama," Sis said. "Always trying to correct folks."

"Y'all be quiet before I leave y'all here," Rock said. "Getting on my nerves already."

Dot looked around with a frown.

"Where Joe at?"

142

"He got to wash up," Rock said. "Papa made him feed the hogs."

Sis crinkled her nose.

"He still gonna stank."

"That's why he's riding in the back," Rock looked at Dot. "And why you in a hurry? You ain't playing."

"I'm just ready to go," she said.

"Go to who?" Sis asked with a grin.

"You make me sick," Dot replied.

Dot heard the screen door slam. Joe stumbled down the steep concrete steps then slammed into the back of the truck.

"Damn!" Rock exclaimed. "You alright?"

"Yeah!" Joe said as he rubbed his arm.

The truck shook as Joe climbed into the bed. Dot peeked in the back. Rock pressed the clutch, turned the key and the old truck rumbled away, belching puffs of black smoke to signal its presence. They bounced over the rough patch on the dirt road then sped between the dormant cornfields and by the hog pen, the putrid aroma sparking a frown on their faces. Rock shifted gears and sped down the smooth stretch of dirt, slowing down a bit as they crossed the railroad tracks running across the entry to the farm road. He jerked the steering wheel to the left as they entered Macon Road, Dot squealing as Sis leaned into her.

"Get your big self off me," Dot said in mock anger.

"You need to gain about twenty pounds," Sis snapped. "Maybe that yella boy you like would take a look at you then."

Dot pressed her lips together so as not to cuss Sis out.

"What yella boy? Rock asked.

"You know," Sis answered. "That Peterson boy, the tall one with the curly hair."

"You talking about Big Tom?"

"That's the one."

Rock laughed. "Get in line, Dot. Just about every woman in the valley after that one. He's a good ball-player, too. Wouldn't be surprised if the Atlanta Crackers sent a scout to take a look at him."

Dot became worried for no reason. It wasn't like Tom leaving was going to change her life either way.

"You think he'd take it if they did?" she asked. "You didn't."

"I make more money selling hogs than what they pay," Rock said. "I don't know about Big Tom, though. He ain't been doing much since he got back from Germany."

"What a Negro doing in Germany?" Sis asked.

"He was in the army," Rock answered. "Went there right after the war. When he came back his daddy had sold their farm and moved to Columbus."

"I wish pappa would sell our farm," Sis said. "I'm tired of living in the country."

"Then what you gonna do?" Dot asked. "That farm is the only reason you big as you is. Sitting around eating all day."

Dot expected Sis to respond, but she just laughed.

"I guess I better find me a good job or a better man then," she said.

The three of them laughed as they rolled down the road into the city. It was good to have the day off to spend with folks their age. Papa used to drive them to the games before Rock got his own car. Dot didn't care that much for baseball, but she did enjoy time away from mama and papa. They were always correcting her and teaching her, or she was ironing and washing clothes. Mama said she had more common sense than the others but was too hard-headed for her own good. Papa said she was the smartest of their twelve children and should go

to college like her other brothers and sisters. She would
make a fine teacher, he would say. Dot didn't want to be
a teacher. She didn't know exactly what she wanted. But
for the time being, she just wanted Big Tom to notice
her.

The parking spaces by the old baseball field were almost full when they arrived. Rock found the closest
space to the diamond. No sooner did he park did Joe
clamber out of the bed, trip and fall onto the pavement.
Rock climbed out of the cabin, shaking his head.

"Boy, you as clumsy as a drunk chicken," he said.

"Yeah, but I can run them bases," Joe said.

"That you can," Rock admitted. "Although I don't
know how."

Sis and Dot got out of the truck. Sis immediately began primping, adjusting her dress and fluffing her hair.
She opened her pouch and took out a lipstick tube. Dot's
eyes went wide.

"What you staring at?" Sis asked. "You need to be
asking me to use it. Your lips are the only thing that ain't
skinny about you. Boys like that."

"I ain't worried about what 'boys' like," Dot said.
"You better make sure you get all that off before you get
home. Papa sees one speck and he gonna have a fit."

"Shoot, I ain't worried about papa out here, and you
shouldn't either," Sis said. "Come over here."

Dot stepped away. "What?"

Sis grabbed her arm and pulled her close. "Girl, come
on over here."

Sis aimed the lipstick at Dot. Dot cringed and turned
her head away. Sis frowned, dropping her hand to her
hips.

"Come on now girl! You want Big Tom to see you,
right? Ain't no way he's gonna miss those big red lips."

"Okay," she said. "But don't let me forget to take it off."

Sis grinned. "That's more like it!"

Dot closed her eyes. The lipstick pressing against her lips felt like sin.

"There!" Sis said.

Dot hurried to the rear-view mirror of the truck to see.

"Lord Jesus," she whispered.

She was reaching into her purse to get a handkerchief to wipe it off when Sis grabbed her arm and began dragging her toward the field.

"Come on! Let's get a good seat so Big Tom can see you!"

Sis grabbed Dot's hand and they fast walked to the hill overlooking the baseball field. Sis pushed her way to the best spot, ignoring the nasty looks and words from the other folks. Dot apologized the best she could while Sis spread the old quilt blanket out for them to sit. Dot dropped their picnic basket then shaded her eyes with her hand as she stared at the dugout. The boys from Seale, Alabama were sitting on their side, ribbing each other as they always did before a game.

"I don't see him," she said.

"Maybe he ain't coming," Sis said.

"He better," Dot replied. "If he doesn't, them Seale boys gonna get they asses whupped."

A loud bang made everyone jump. Heads turned to see an old Chevy pickup chug into the parking lot, belching and banging like an old cow. The truck jerked still then the driver's door swung open.

Big Tom Peterson wriggled out of the truck, then stretched. Dot's eyes went soft as she took him all in; a head full of black curly hair, pencil thin mustache resting on his top lip. He grinned at the Seale Boys bench, showing a single gold tooth among his bright even teeth. Tom

reached through the window, grabbed his glove then trotted to the bench.

"Mm, mm, mm," Sis said.

Dot spun about and glared at her sister. Sis fell over
laughing.

"I'm just playing with you, girl. I don't want that
man. I like my men dark brown like chocolate. But it
ain't like he yours, and he ain't never gonna be if you
don't talk to him."

"I will," Dot whispered. "One day."

Sis cupped her hands around her mouth.

"Big Tom!" she shouted.

Dot knocked her hands down.

"Girl! You crazy!"

When Dot looked up, Big Tom was looking straight at
her. Her eyes met his, and her mouth opened slightly.
Tom squinted as if trying to make her out. One of his
friends dropped a heavy hand on his shoulder then
guided him away.

"That was your chance," Sis said. "So much for that."

Dot packed her basket then stomped away.

"Hey, where you going? At least leave the food!"

Dot made her way back to the truck. She opened the
door then sat and folded her arms across her chest.

"She makes me sick!" she said aloud. "Next time
I'ma punch her in her smart-ass mouth!"

Dot jumped out the truck and paced. As she calmed,
she came back to her senses. She wasn't going to punch
Sis in the mouth. If she hit her sister every time she said
something stupid or embarrassing, she'd be punching her
all the time. 'She don't know no better,' mama always
said. Dot didn't believe that, but she knew Sis was who
she was, just like all of them were.

Sis was right about one thing. She would never talk to
Tom. And if she did, Tom would most likely not talk to

her. She was plain, she was skinny, and she didn't have a way with words like Sis. She was smart and she was strong, but she ain't never heard a man say that about any woman he liked. Well, at least not her brothers.

Dot lingered around the truck while the game took place. She nibbled on her sandwich and sipped from her thermos, turning her head toward the game whenever there was a loud roar. She climbed back into the truck then leaned back against the seat, listening to the sounds of the game before dozing off.

"Hey!"

Dot jumped upright. Rock looked through the driver's side window, a big grin on his face.

"You been here the whole time?"

Dot wiped her mouth. "Almost."

"Damn girl, you missed it!"

Sis scampered up beside Rock then threw her arm around his shoulder.

"Rock was throwing stingers! Them Seale boys were swinging at air all day."

Dot grinned. "What was the score?"

"Five to nothing," Rock said. "A no-hitter!"

"Your boy Tom left in a bad mood," Sis said.

"Stop calling him that," Dot said. "He ain't my boy."

Sis grinned. "Your. Boy."

"Sis!" Dot shouted.

Dot stomped toward Sis, her hands rolled into fists. Sis jumped behind Rock.

"Don't let her hit me!" she squealed.

Rock grabbed Dot, pushing her arms to her side.

"Leave Sis alone," he said. "Everybody knows she crazy."

Sis glared the back of Rock's head.

"What?"

148

Rock ignored her. "Besides, you don't need to be messing with Tom. Them Seale boys ain't no good."

"You ain't my daddy," Dot said. "I told you I don't like that boy."

Dot spun around and marched back to the truck.

"Let's go home." Rock said.

Dot didn't get into the truck cab. She opened the gate and scrambled into the bed.

"Girl, what you doing?" Sis asked. "Get on in here."

Dot didn't say anything.

"Come on, girl," Sis said. "I'm sorry."

"You always sorry," Dot shot back.

"Leave her alone," Rock said.

He took Sis's arm and led her away. Dot watched them climb into the cab then turned away. She didn't even want to look at the back of Sis's head.

Joe sauntered to the truck, ignoring the open gate. He climbed over the side of the truck bed then fell onto the surface. His head hit the wood and he laughed. Dot leaned close to him then jerked back as the combination of alcohol, sweat funk and hog pen aroma assaulted her. She almost changed her mind about riding in the cab.

"Them Seale boys know how to have a good time," he slurred.

"You better sober your butt up before we get home," Dot said.

Joe looked up.

"What you doing back here?"

"Sis."

Joe chuckled. "She musta really got on your last nerve if you back here with my stank ass."

Dot laughed. "At least you know you stank. I hope Rock drives fast."

Joe pulled Dot into a hug and Dot screamed.

"Now you smell like me," he said.

They laughed as Rock drove off. Joe was a mess, but he was fun. They settled down, Dot enjoying the wind blowing against her and rustling her hair. For those few minutes, she felt free, nothing but the sound of the road and the passing pines. She wished life could be like this all the time. No chores, no worries, no judgement, no unfairness.

Those thoughts dissipated as they crossed the railroad tracks. Dot glanced to the right, looking at the lone shack on the edge of papa's farm and a chill hit her despite the late summer heat. Miss Caldonia lived there, the root woman. Though she'd resided there as long as Dot could remember, she'd never been to her house. Every time she gazed in the direction mama would slap her hand and scold her.

"Don't be looking up there," she would say. "Ain't nothing up there but trouble."

Not everybody felt the same. Miss Caldonia had healed sicknesses the white doctors couldn't or wouldn't treat. She was also one of the two colored midwives in Midland, which meant she'd delivered most of the Negro children around until the hospitals started accepting Negroes. There was something else Miss Caldonia was famous or infamous for, depending on a person's point of view. There were whispers that for the right price, Miss Caldonia could concoct a love potion. She could stir a brew that would make any man fall in love with any woman, and the other way around, too. That was just wrong, Dot thought. What's the use to being married to someone that didn't love you because they wanted to? Would you have to keep giving them the potion to keep them? And why was she thinking about it?

Mama was standing outside the house with a grim look as Rock parked the truck behind the house near the barn.

"About time y'all got back," she said. "Too much work to do around here for y'all to be playing."

Dot and the others climbed out of the truck. Sis flashed her a smile and Dot smiled back despite herself. As annoying as Sis could be, she was her baby sister. Besides, her mind was on other things. She had to visit Miss Caldonia.

* * *

Mama hovered over Dot's bed, a frown on her face. "You too sick to go to church?"

Dot nodded then winced.

"Yes, mama."

"If you sick, the best place for you is at church," Mama said.

Daddy stuck his head in the room.

"Let her rest, Louise," he said. "Won't hurt for her to miss one day of church."

"You tell the Lord that," Mama said.

"C'mon, Louise," Daddy urged. "We got to go. I'm praying at devotion today."

Mama started for the door.

"You wash them breakfast dishes when you start feeling better."

"Yes, ma'am," Dot replied.

Mama left Dot and Sis's room. Dot peeked from under the covers then listened to make sure everyone was gone before she threw the covers back. She was fully dressed except for shoes. She put on her shoes then crawled under the bed for the box she'd hidden a few days ago. Checking the house one last time, Dot crept out the back door, running as fast as she could to Miss Caldonia's front porch. By the time she reached it, she was out of breath and sweating like a mule. She knocked on the door then looked around, hoping no one saw her here.

"Who dat is?" a gravelly voice called out.

"Dorothy Simpson," she replied.

Dot listened to the uneven footfalls grow louder and louder until they stopped and the tarnished brass doorknob turned. Miss Caldonia stepped into the doorway and Dot held back a gasp. She looked much younger than Dot expected. She was heavy around the breasts and hips, the yellow sundress she wore showing its age. Her umber skin was unblemished, her white teeth perfectly set in her small mouth. A pink roller peeked from under her headscarf, revealing jet black hair with strands of gray. Her expression was not pleasant.

"Dot? What you doing over here?" she said.

"You know me?"

Miss Caldonia rolled her eyes. "You live right over there. Get in this house before your mama sees you!"

Miss Caldonia grabbed her wrist with a vise-like grip and yanked her inside. The room was sparsely furnished, just a large sofa and two folding chairs. Two bushels of green peas rested before the sofa. Miss Caldonia sat and began shelling.

"Now why you here?" she asked. "Somebody sick?"

"No, ma'am," Dot said. She was still in awe.

"Well, what you here for?"

Dot swallowed before speaking. "Folks say you can make folks fall in love."

Miss Caldonia chuckled. "Lord have mercy. Who you trying to trap, girl?"

"I ain't trying to trap nobody!" Dot blurted. "I don't even want him to love me. At least not yet. I just want to get to know him."

Miss Caldonia looked up. "So, you just want him to like you."

"I don't even want that. I just want him to see me."

"Um. Who we talking about?"

"Tom Peterson."

Miss Caldonia fell back on her sofa and laughed like she'd just heard the funniest joke ever.

Dot felt her cheeks get warm. "It ain't that funny!" she said.

Miss Caldonia shook her head as she waved her hand.

"I ain't laughing at you, child," she said. "It's just that it's Tom Pete again. If I had a dollar for every time somebody asked me to make Big Tom notice them, I'd be the richest Negro woman in Muscogee County."

"So, you can't do it?" Dot asked.

"Depends. Come here."

Dot tipped over to the sofa and sat beside her. She smelled like peppermint and mothballs.

"Give me your hand," Miss Caldonia said.

Dot put out her hand and Miss Caldonia took it. Her calloused skin felt rough against Dot's palm, yet her touch was comforting. Miss Caldonia stared at her palm.

"Good lines," she said.

She slid her hand up to Dot's wrist then closed her eyes. When she opened them, she smiled.

"You got a good heart, too."

Miss Caldonia stood then shuffled out of the room. Dot heard clamoring pots then silence. When Miss Caldonia returned, she was holding a burlap bag.

"Go to the woods down by Little Uchee and fill this here with muscadines. Once it's full, bring it back to me."

"But I brought you some of daddy's sugar cane to pay," Dot said.

Miss Caldonia grinned as a faraway look took over her face.

"Your daddy always been sweet," she said. "Sweet like candy."

Dot frowned. "How you know my daddy?"

"Take this bag and go," Miss Caldonia replied. "And don't come back until it's full."

"But . . ."

Miss Caldonia grasped Dot's shoulder then spun her toward the door. She then placed her palms against Dot's back and pushed her.

"Go on now," she said. "And leave that sugar cane."

"Yes, ma'am," Dot said.

She fumbled with the doorknob. Miss Caldonia reached around her, opening the door.

"Go on now," she urged.

Dot tipped across the porch and downstairs. As soon as she heard the door close, she sprinted home, clutching the bag to her chest. She hurried through the house to her room then concealed the bag where she hid the sugar cane. Dot undressed then put on her house dress before going to the kitchen to finish the dishes. She was washing the last plate when papa entered the house with mama close on his heels.

"I see you feeling better," mama said.

"Yes, ma'am, I am," Dot said.

"Good. Since you couldn't bring yourself to church today, I need you to go out to the field and pick three bushels of lima beans for supper."

Dot tried hard to hide her joy. The lima bean field was near the woods where the muscadines grew. She couldn't have thought of a better punishment. Dot lowered her head as she put on her best sad face.

"Yes, ma'am."

"Why you punishing her?" Papa said. "Girl can't help being sick."

Dot felt a twinge of guilt. Papa was defending her lie.

Mama walked out of the kitchen. "I ain't studying you. She better have those beans ready for dinner."

Papa followed Mama out of the kitchen to their room at the end of the hall, the two of them fussing all the way down the hall. Dot finished the dishes then went to her room. She was reaching for the burlap bag under her bed when she heard her door open. She rolled her eyes.

"What you want, Sis?"

Dot tucked the bag under her dress before standing. Sis was standing there with a skeptical look on her plump face.

"You wasn't really sick, was you?" she asked.

"I was sick enough," Dot snapped. She was still mad at Sis.

"I'll help you pick beans," Sis said.

"NO! . . . I mean no," Dot said. "I don't want to be bothered with you right now."

"I said I was sorry!" Sis said.

"Sorry didn't do it. You did," Dot replied.

She brushed by Sis, hoping she wouldn't be her usual persistent self. Dot grabbed the empty baskets on the back porch, scampered down the stairs then followed the path that ran between the cornfield and the chicken coop to the hedgerow, dividing the back fields from the front. Papa and mama grew watermelons, black-eyed peas, and lima beans on these acres. A smaller hog pen sat at the edge of the lima bean field, which ended at the boundary of the woods that held the muscadines.

Dot balanced the baskets on her head as she strolled to the field. She stopped at the hedges, picking a few late blackberries and popping them into her mouth. They were still sweet. She'd have to remember to stop and pick a few more on the way back to the house.

The hogs lounged in their mud, the stench pushing Dot away and forcing her to cover her nose. A few more minutes of walking and she skipped alongside rows and rows of lima beans. She kept walking until she reached the woods. After looking to make sure she wasn't seen, she stepped into the thicket. It didn't take her long to find the patch of muscadines, the thick vines intertwined around a group of oaks. There were more than enough to fill her bag. In minutes she was done, with plenty of time to pick enough beans for supper.

The family gathered for dinner. Papa gave a mini sermon to bless the food and they ate, Dot tickled by the raucous bantering between her brothers, with Sis always trying to get in a word.

"Dot, what you over there grinning about?" Rock asked.

"Nothing," Dot replied. She didn't realize she had been smiling the whole time. It was hope that caused it, the chance that whatever Miss Caldonia was about to do was going to help Tommy Pete see her.

"She probably over there thinking about Tommy Pete," Sis said.

And just like that her good mood was snatched away. Dot pushed her chair away from the table and stood.

"I ain't hungry no more," she said. "Can I go to my room?"

Mama looked her up and down.

"Go on," she said. "You might as well wash up, too."

Dot picked up her plate, heading out back to scrap it into the slop barrel. She returned to the kitchen, washed her plate and set it on the counter. By the time everyone else was done eating, Dot had washed up and was in the bed, reading her book by Langston Hughes. She heard a tap on her door.

"Leave me alone, Sis," she said.

"I was just . . ."

"Go on, girl. Just go."

Dot smiled as Sis stomped away. She put down her book, climbed out of bed and checked her muscadine stash.

"Now what in the world is a bunch of muscadines gonna do for me?" she whispered. Only Miss Caldonia could answer that question.

* * *

Three days went by before she had a chance to sneak back to Miss Caldonia's house. When the woman answered the door, she looked the same as she did when Dot visited before, except this time she greeted Dot with a kind smile.

"Come on in, sugar," she said.

Dot followed Miss Caldonia to the sofa. The bushels were gone, replaced by a low coffee table with a scratched surface. On top of the table were two metal buckets.

"Pour them muscadines in them pails," she said.

"Yes, ma'am,"

Dot poured the wild grapes into the buckets while Miss Caldonia plopped down onto her sofa.

"Now come sit next to me and let's mash these bullets."

Miss Caldonia stuck her hand into the pail before her and began mashing muscadines. Dot watched her for a moment then did the same.

"Miss Caldonia, how you know my daddy?"

Miss Caldonia grinned. "What I'm about to tell you, you can't tell nobody else, you hear me?"

"Yes, ma'am."

"Your daddy used to be sweet on me," she said.

Dot stopped mashing. "What!?!"

"Un hunh," Miss Caldonia said. "And I was sweet on him, too. Who you think built this house?"

"But . . . if daddy was sweet on you, and you was sweet on him, why ain't y'all married?"

Miss Caldonia laughed. "You figure me doing what I do, we should have been married. Let me tell you something, child. When a person comes courting, you want them there because they want to be there."

Dot stopped mashing the muscadines.

"You saying what I'm asking you to do is wrong?"

"I ain't said nothing."

"If you think it's wrong, then why you helping me?"

"Woman got to make a living," Miss Caldonia said. "Besides, you asked me to make Tommy see you. Ain't no harm in that. The rest will be up to you."

"So why didn't you and daddy marry?"

"Because he met your mama and her fast ass," Miss Caldonia said. "She wanted him a lot more than I did and was willing to do a lot more to get him."

Dot laughed. "Ooh wee, mama. I know who Sis takes after now."

Miss Caldonia chuckled. "You take after your daddy. Yes, you do."

She peered into Dot's bucket.

"Okay, that's enough mashing."

Dot looked up. "What's next?"

"Nothing for you," Miss Caldonia replied. "Time for me to get to work. Come on wash your hands."

Dot followed Miss Caldonia to her kitchen sink. She rinsed her hands, then washed them with lye soap.

"Come back in a month and a half," Miss Caldonia said. "Your wine will be ready then. And bring some of those blackberries you like with you. I need to make some pies."

"Yes, ma'am."

Dot left the house with mixed emotions. She did want Tommy to notice her, but would it be real love if it took hoodoo to get his attention? She thought about what Miss Caldonia said about her and daddy, too. What if Tommy did like her because of what Miss Caldonia was going to do? Would it last?

She stopped. Maybe she should go back and tell Miss Caldonia to forget about everything. She'd talk to Tommy in her own time and her own way. She gazed at the house, and her doubt faded. Dot turned around and continued home.

* * *

The weeks crept by like a turtle climbing a steep hill. Dot immersed herself into the day routines and rhythms of the farm to keep her mind off Miss Caldonia. She eventually made up with Sis, although she knew they would eventually fall out again over something Sis would say without thinking. One thing Dot didn't do was go to the games. Instead, she spent the time doing chores with mama (there were always chores to do with mama) or picking blackberries. Their sweetness calmed her and sitting against a thick oak tree near the woods was always soothing.

School was coming soon. Dot graduated from high school two years ago and talk of college buzzed throughout the house. Her older sister Ventrine and brother Donald were both in college, Savannah State and Albany State respectively, and daddy was asking her what she wanted to do. He and mama were determined their children got opportunities they didn't, and they believed that started with the best education farming could buy. But Dot couldn't make up her mind what she wanted to do. She was going back and forth between teaching and

nursing, but she didn't have a passion for either. But like
Ventrine said, passion is something for people that have
a choice, something that a Negro woman in Muscogee
County had little of.

Dot finished the dinner dishes with a little sunlight remaining. She grabbed her sweater then went for a quick
walk to the woods. She frowned as she passed the hedge-
rows; blackberry season was over, and she'd have to
wait until next summer to enjoy them. The bean fields
were filled and almost ready to harvest, which meant
busy mornings and evenings in the days ahead. She
reached the end of the fields. Her favorite spot, the ancient white oak, was changing colors, yellow leaves scattered among the green canopy. As she neared, she
noticed a small burlap bag near the trunk. Dot squatted
then picked up the bag. She opened it; inside was a green
glass bottle sealed with a cork. A piece of folded paper
was inside as well. Dot put down the bag and opened the
paper.

Here's your wine. Give it to him after the game.
That's when those Seale boys like to drink. Good luck.
Caldonia

Dot hands trembled as she lifted the bottle again. She
was tempted to open it up, pour out the wine and forget
the whole thing. If that boy didn't notice her on his own,
he wasn't worth the time, she thought. She sat against
the tree, the muscadine wine in her lap. She closed her
eyes and tried to image her future. Would she spend the
rest of her life on the farm, tending the fields and taking
care of mama and daddy when they got old? Would she
go off to college, get her degree, then leave Midland for
Savannah, or maybe even Atlanta? Or would she go to

the baseball game next weekend, give Big Tom this bottle of hoodoo and let it do its work?

When Saturday rolled around, Dot had made her decision. She spent most of the day fixing her hair, then pressed her best dress. When she walked down the stairs to the truck, Sis's eyes went wide.

"Ooooh! Look at you!" she said.

Rock looked her up and down then frowned.

"Where you going?

Dot brushed by both of them then climbed into the truck cab. She was nervous and ready to leave. If mama or daddy saw her dressed up like this, she'd have some explaining to do. The bottle of muscadine wine was wrapped tight in her sitting blanket. She still wasn't sure if she was going to give it to Big Tom. Once he drank it, there was no turning back.

"Where's Joe at?" Dot said. "He needs to come on."

Mama came from around the front of the house and Dot's throat went dry. She lowered her head and pushed back into the seat as much as she could. Sis glanced at her, then sat up, blocking mama's view.

"Hey, mama!" Sis said. "We're going to the game!"

Mama sucked her teeth. "I know. Y'all be ready to fold some clothes when you get back."

"Yes, ma'am," Sis chirped.

Dot stayed small until Sis touched her shoulder.

"She's gone now," she said.

Dot straightened, quickly searching for her forever late brother.

"Where the . . ."

The truck shook as Joe climbed into the bed.

"Let's go!" he shouted. "I'm ready to kick them Seale boys' butt!"

Rock pulled off and Dot relaxed. Her eyes kept drifting down her blanket and the hidden present inside.

161

"Let me put some makeup on you," Sis said.

Dot looked at her sister and smiled. She was being so nice. She probably suspected what Dot was up to, but she didn't know all of it.

"Okay," Dot replied.

Sis took out her makeup kit and went to work.

"I like it when you're not mad at me," she said.

"Then stop making me mad," Dot replied.

"I can't promise that," Sis said as she applied rouge to Dot's cheeks.

"I know," Dot replied.

Sis was done by the time they pulled into the parking lot. Rock and Joe hesitated, both staring at Dot.

"What?" Dot said.

They shook their heads then headed for the field, whispering and laughing.

Sis and Dot went to the spectator hill and sat. Sis spread out her blanket, but Dot kept hers rolled up. A few minutes later the Seale Boys appeared. Big Tom towered over the others, sauntering to the dugout with his bat resting on his shoulders. A few of the women yelled out his name but he didn't take notice. Once he entered the dugout, they broke out their bottles of moonshine and the game began. Dot bit her lip as she watched Big Tom take a healthy swig. By the end of the game the last thing he was going to want was something else to drink. But she had come this far; she might as well go all the way.

She was so distracted with her thoughts that she didn't notice when the game ended. Sis shook her shoulder.

"Come on, girl. It's time to go."

Dot jumped. "Wha . . . What!?!?"

Dot clambered to her feet. Big Tom strolled to his truck, exchanging words with his friends while ignoring the women ogling him and calling his name.

"I got to go," Dot said.

She fast-walked across the field to the dirt parking lot. Tom was fumbling with his keys, trying to unlock his door. Dot walked faster.

"Excuse me," she said.

Tom opened his door then reached inside his truck.

"Tom!" she shouted.

Tom looked up and their eyes met. He smirked, then stepped away from the truck. He had a small box in his hand. Dot unraveled her blanket, revealing the bottle of muscadine wine. By the time they reached each other, both were grinning.

Dot gave Tom the bottle. Tom gave her the box.

"Muscadine wine?" Tom said.

Dot nodded then lifted the box lid.

"Blackberries," Dot said.

They laughed out loud.

"That woman ain't got no hoodoo magic," Tom said.

Dot shook her head. "Yes, she does. She got both of us standing here in spite of ourselves."

"Come on, Dot!" Rock yelled. "We got to go!"

"See you at the next game?" Tom asked.

"Yeah," Dot replied. "I'll be there."

Dot walked backwards for a minute, then turned and skipped back to the truck. Rock shook his head.

"Well, I'll be damned," he said. "A Seale boy."

"Shut up and get in the truck," Sis said. "That's Dot's boyfriend, not yours."

Dot hopped into the cab. There were so many things that she wasn't certain of, but there was one thing that was sure. She loved muscadines and she loved this sunny day. Yes, she did.

Muscadine Wine

About The Author

Milton Davis is an award winning Black Speculative fiction author and owner of MVmedia, LLC, a publishing company specializing in Science Fiction and Fantasy based on African/African Diaspora history, culture, and traditions. Milton is the author of twenty-six novels and short story collections and editor/co-editor of ten anthologies. His short stories have appeared in several anthologies and magazines, most notably Black Panther: Tales of Wakanda; Slay: Stories of the Vampire Noire; Obsidian Literature and Arts in the African Diaspora, and Tales from the Magician's Skull. Milton's story 'The Swarm' was nominated for the 2017 British Science Fiction Association Award for Short Fiction and his story, Carnival, was nominated for the 2020 British Science Fiction Association Award for Short Fiction. He is a recipient of the 2022 East Coast Black Age of Comics Convention Pioneer Lifetime Achievement Award.

For more novels by Milton J. Davis, visit MVmedia, LLC, the best of the Black Fantastic!

The first historical fiction novel by Milton J. Davis takes place in 15th century East Africa and Japan! Swahili merchant Kesi Masanja (Black Rose) takes responsibility for Danuja Tanaka after her family is killed by rival daimyos. Together they navigate the challenges of their societies while struggling with the legacies of their families.

For nearly twenty years corporate security cyborg Carlos
Mejia has lived a life of danger and privilege in the United
Cities. But one day he receives a life-changing contact. The
corporation that employed him and funded his tech has gone
bankrupt, and now he is an asset to be collected and liqui-
dated! Desperate to stay alive, Carlos seeks the help of street
hacker Michelle Carter to dump his tech and become 'normal.'
What they discover is a conspiracy that threatens to set the
United Cities on a destructive path . . . unless they stop it.

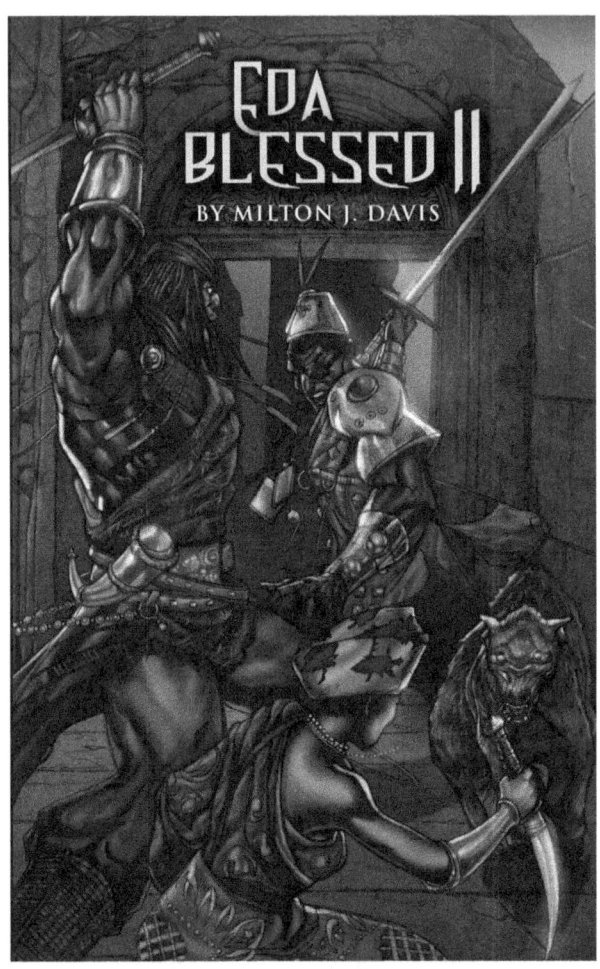

Omari Ket's adventures continue in Eda Blessed II. A collection of ten new tales span Omari's indentured service with the Mikijen to his journeys as a freelance mercenary. Omari fights, lies and runs his way across Ki Khanga, guided by an unknown destiny and protected by Eda.